I0638701

The Last Conversation

Soraya Radfield

Published by Soraya Radfield, 2025.

THE LAST CONVERSATION

First edition. May 15, 2025.

Copyright © 2025 Soraya Radfield.

ISBN: 978-1764102810

Written by Soraya Radfield.

Table of Contents

Author's Note

D ear Reader,
   Thank you for walking this path with me.

The Last Conversation is my first novel—and I'll admit, I didn't see it coming. Writing wasn't something I had always planned. But somewhere between the silence and the story, I found a passion I didn't expect. And it caught me—quietly, completely.

This book began with a feeling, not a plot. An ache, really. A sense that some stories live not in the noise, but in the pause. In what we remember when the world forgets. In what we choose to carry forward. And how silence isn't emptiness, but an archive of everything we were too afraid to say out loud.

As I wrote, I found myself drawing from the things I've always loved—history, architecture, memory, surveillance, music, trust, betrayal. This novel gave me the joy and deep satisfaction of weaving all those fragments into something whole. Something human.

Hannah, Ethan, and Jacob are not just characters. They're keepers of the question that lingers when the truth feels too dangerous to tell. They taught me that silence is not absence—it's an archive. And legacy isn't what we leave behind. It's how we're remembered by those who listened.

If this story stayed with you—if it made you pause, reflect, or feel something slow and unnamed—then it has done what I hoped it would.

Let me know your thoughts on my webpage: Amazon site.

Thank you for listening.
Until the next echo,
Soraya Radfield

Prologue

Undated Archive Fragment — Location: Unknown (later revealed to be Istanbul)

"If you're hearing this, then you've found the first thread."

His voice was steady. Not hurried. Not fearful. It moved with the kind of clarity that came from knowing the end had already begun.

"This isn't a confession. It's a conversation. One that started long before I left—and one that will keep speaking after I'm gone."

A soft rustle—paper, perhaps. Then the scrape of a chair. He inhaled, the sound low, reflective.

"There are places in history where sound bends. Where meaning isn't written but played. Cedrela was one of those places. Ottoman minds hid it in architecture, in silence, in song. And someone—someone with reach—is trying to erase it."

Hannah adjusted the volume. The device crackled faintly. The room she sat in was quiet, but the air around her felt sharpened—like it too was listening.

"I kept you out of it for as long as I could," he said softly, his voice layered with a weight she'd never heard before—regret tangled with love, tenderness shadowed by quiet desperation. "I never wanted you to carry this danger. But they found me." His breath caught briefly, raw and trembling with something unsaid, something long held back. "And I realised—it can't stay buried any longer. It has to be decoded. It has to be you."

There was a silence, a hesitation delicate enough to hold an entire history.

"You always heard what I didn't say," he whispered, the words fracturing slightly at the edges, a single heartbreaking crack that slipped through, revealing the depth of everything he'd left unspoken until now.

"This is our last conversation, Han. But not the last truth. The rest... the rest is scattered. Follow it. Not for me. For what we were trying to remember before the world forgot how."

A final breath. Then silence. No click. No goodbye. Just absence.

And somewhere beyond that silence, truth began to stir.

"If they extract it from the structure, they'll never understand the cost. They'll echo the ghost, not the grief. Cedrela... isn't silence. It's what silence guards."

—Only the wind. And the faint, persistent echo of a melody that didn't want to be forgotten.

Chapter One - When Everything Changed

It began with a single, chilling message.

"Trust no one. Not even me."

Hannah stared blankly at her phone screen, the words glowing ominously like the last flickering light in a darkened room, their unsettling presence hanging over her like an approaching storm. The message, an unexpected whisper from Ethan, her typically steadfast husband, felt dissonant and wrong in every conceivable way. She wrapped her cardigan tightly around herself, seeking warmth against the biting October breeze that gusted through Istanbul's amber-lit streets, where rustling leaves whispered haunting tales of endings yet to come.

She cast her gaze toward the Bosphorus, where the sun began to spill golden light across the water, a sight that once bore witness to the imperial fleet of Sultan Mehmed the Conqueror during the 15th century—a shimmering reminder of ambition, power, and Istanbul's enduring identity as the bridge between two continents. With each passing moment, sunlight pierced the misty veil of dawn, blissfully ignorant of the chaos erupted within her.

Her heart raced, a wild beast trapped within the confines of her chest, each frantic beat echoing painfully in her ears. Ethan had always been the steady rock in her life—meticulous, predictable, unwavering. Yet he had never been cryptic. This was a jarring departure from the man she knew. This couldn't be Ethan—could it?

With trembling fingers, she dialed his number, her mind swirling with dread that coiled tighter around her stomach with each unanswered ring. A robotic voice cut sharply through her rising panic: "The number you are trying to reach is unavailable."

A flash of memory surged unbidden into her mind: Ethan at their dinner two nights ago, laughter spilling between them like rich wine, his dark eyes glimmering with a warmth that felt like home, his hand sliding across the table to clasp hers in an affectionate gesture. That moment had been so blissfully ordinary, so reassuringly safe, and yet now it felt like a faded photograph from another life, the colors bleeding and the edges curling. Confusion thickened the air around her, twisting with the mounting panic in her chest. Had she overlooked a sign, some subtle indication that all was not well? Was Ethan concealing something monumental from her? The uncertainty gnawed at her insides, steadily transforming her concern into dread. It felt incomprehensible that he could simply vanish overnight, yet the deafening silence on the other end of the phone screamed louder than any confirmation of his absence ever could.

Out on the streets, the city came alive, a tapestry of life and energy, untouched and oblivious to her turmoil. She was isolated in her spiraling terror, a solitary figure engulfed by shadows. Hannah's breathing quickened, each breath participating in her spiraling descent into despair. The truth struck her as inescapable: she needed help. Yet there was only one person who could possibly provide it now—Jacob, her estranged brother, a man whose voice had faded into the background of her memories, the silence between them a chasm filled with unresolved hurt.

Swallowing hard, she hesitated, finger hovering over his name, the weight of years passed pressing down on her. Each ring magnified her anxiety, a countdown to an uncertain reunion, until the call connected with a hesitant voice—tired, guarded, yet undeniably Jacob.

"Hannah?"

She paused, a tidal wave of old pain and anger threatening to drown her.

"Jacob, Ethan's gone. And I think he's in danger."

There were no hello, how are you nor any pleasantries exchanged between them. There was a profound silence, heavy with unspoken truths, guilt, and the burden of countless wounds left to fester.

"Tell me everything."

With that, their lives shifted irreversibly, pulling them into a vortex of secrets neither was prepared to confront. Yet amidst the silence of years and the jagged edges of their fractured relationship, something ancient and unspoken stirred between them—blood ties, stubborn and resilient. Because sometimes, when the world crumbles around you, even the most fractured bonds can transform into a lifeline.

Blood, after all, is thicker than water.

—Not every silence is a pause. Some are traps.

Chapter Two - Threads Unraveling

The late-morning sun filtered through a veil of amber leaves, casting golden reflections across the Bosphorus. Ferries moved lazily between continents, their horns low and distant, like weary sighs over the water. Autumn in Istanbul wasn't harsh—it crept in with elegance. The air had that clean crispness, sharp enough to stir old memories but soft enough to lull you into a false sense of calm.

Hannah stood at the kitchen window, fingers wrapped around a mug of lukewarm coffee she'd forgotten to sip. Below, the narrow streets of Bebek curved along the shoreline like a secret too winding to follow. The scent of roasted chestnuts drifted up from a vendor's cart, mingling with the salty tang of the sea. Normally, these little details grounded her—the colours, the sounds, the rituals of daily life. Today, they felt like static, faint echoes of a world that no longer fit.

Inside, the apartment wore the aftermath of a sleepless night. An open book lay on its spine beside the couch. Ethan's sweater—still draped over the armrest—held the faintest trace of his cologne. The air felt suspended, like everything had stopped breathing with her.

She checked her phone again. No message. No update. Nothing.

The silence pressed against her chest.

A knock at the door startled her.

Hannah's pulse kicked up. She hesitated, the phone still clutched in her hand as if it could shield her from whatever news awaited on the other side. Another knock—firmer this time. Familiar, even after all these years.

She opened the door.

Jacob stood there—taller than she remembered, though maybe it was just the heaviness he carried now. His trench coat, creased and weathered at the collar, flapped gently in the breeze. Beneath it, a charcoal sweater peeked out, fraying slightly at the cuffs. His eyes—once sharp with certainty—looked older, shadowed, maybe even apologetic. But still unmistakably his.

He held out a paper tray with two cups of steaming coffee.

"Double shot, no sugar—for you. And black for me," he said, voice low.

She blinked, caught off guard. "You remembered."

"Some things don't get erased. No matter how much time passes."

The warmth of the cup seeped into her fingers. She hadn't realised how cold she was until that moment. As she stepped aside to let him in, a gust of sea air curled-in behind him, dragging the smell of roasted chestnuts and rain-slick stone.

Jacob crossed the threshold slowly, his boots quiet on the hardwood. The scent of the apartment—lemongrass from a half-burned candle, and something distinctly Ethan—hit him like a wave. He'd never said it aloud, but he'd admired Ethan. Envied him, even. The way he brought steadiness to Hannah's life, the way he'd built something from precision, not fire. It wasn't lost on Jacob how much steadiness he'd failed to offer her himself.

He glanced around, eyes catching every detail. The room hadn't changed much—her love for Ottoman textiles, the carefully

7

arranged bookshelves, the subtle traces of chaos from a sleepless night. But she had changed. More poised. More brittle. The kind of strength forged in silence and stitched together by necessity.

The apartment felt smaller suddenly, more intimate with him in it. Jacob scanned the room instinctively—an old habit from his reporting days. Nothing escaped his gaze. Not the teacup on the table, still half full. Not the sweater draped casually over the arm of the couch. Not the faint lines of tension etched between Hannah's brows.

"It's been a while," he said, setting his satchel by the door.

She managed a dry smile. "Not long enough, some might say."

His lips twitched at the corner, but he didn't smile. "You okay?"

She shook her head. "No."

He nodded once. Not as an answer, but as acknowledgment. Then, gently, he reached over and tucked a strand of hair behind her ear. She flinched, not from him, but from the unfamiliar tenderness. It reminded her of a time when she was twelve and he was fifteen, when she'd scraped her knee on their driveway and he'd torn the sleeve off his shirt to bandage it. They'd buried that memory along with so many others. But it surfaced now, raw and unexpected.

He hadn't come to be forgiven. He'd come because blood had memory. And some debts didn't dissolve just because the years had.

He pulled a slim notebook from his coat. "Start from the beginning."

They sat opposite each other, a low table between them, the coffee cooling slowly as the hours pressed in.

Neither moved much. The apartment felt quieter with Jacob in it—not emptier, but settled in a way that made the silence feel earned. As if the space had finally decided to stop bracing itself and just breathe.

Hannah curled her legs beneath her, wrapping her cardigan tighter around her frame. Jacob sat with his elbows on his knees, fingers laced, watching the grain of the floorboards rather than her face.

The late-morning light shifted across the wall, golden but beginning to fade toward early afternoon. It filtered in through sheer linen curtains, softening the edges of everything, like the city was trying to be kind.

The room held Ethan. Not just his scent or the way his books remained open where he'd left them, but in the way the light fell across the far wall—just how he liked it when he read. In the little imperfections: the blanket not quite folded, the pair of glasses still perched on the side table. His absence didn't yet feel like loss. It felt like a pause. As if at any moment, the door might open and he'd walk in, slightly late, slightly smug, holding some new story she didn't yet know she needed.

Jacob glanced up. "He ever talk to you about disappearing?"

The question landed gently, but it knocked something loose in her.

She blinked. Once. Twice. Her eyes were wide—not wild, but wounded. A calm sadness wrapped tight around something much older. Her grip on the coffee cup shifted; her knuckles whitened for half a second before she exhaled and spoke.

"No," she said. Her voice was even, but it carried the tremor of someone speaking through the centre of a bruise. "He didn't believe in leaving without explanation. Even his silences had structure."

Jacob nodded as if that made sense. "Then maybe this isn't a disappearance. Maybe it's a message."

She looked at him now, eyes narrowing slightly—not out of anger, but focus. There was something grounding in hearing that from Jacob. It didn't fix anything. But it gave shape to the uncertainty.

"You didn't like him at first," she said.

"I didn't trust him," Jacob replied. "He was... too perfect. Like he'd already figured everything out and was just waiting for the rest of us to catch up."

"And then?"

Jacob's gaze wandered to the glass balcony door. The Bosphorus shimmered beyond it, lazy and bright, interrupted only by the slow ferry crossing east to west.

"And then I realised he wasn't perfect. He was careful. There's a difference."

Hannah leaned into the couch cushions, the fabric rising around her. She remembered Ethan meeting Jacob for the first time — the quietness, the studied kindness. How he never pushed her to reconcile, but never encouraged the distance either.

"Ethan believed people always circled back to where they came from," she said softly. "Eventually."

Jacob gave a half-smile. "And yet, he left."

A quiet beat passed. Not bitter. Just honest.

"I don't think he left us," Hannah said after a moment. "I think he's leading us."

Jacob studied her face — pale in the light, tired but determined. It reminded him of the girl who used to read poetry to herself in the corners of their childhood home. The one who always asked harder questions than the world had answers for.

"You always had more faith than me," he said.

"No," she replied. "I just held on to it longer."

—"Then dont let them use his silence against him."

Chapter Three - Secrets Beneath the Surface

The apartment felt different with Jacob in it. Not unsafe—just altered. His energy changed the space, sharpening its edges. While Hannah moved through the living room with purpose, Jacob stood still for a moment, scanning the room as if it were a crime scene.

"Where did he keep his private notes?" Jacob asked.

Hannah gestured toward the bookshelf near Ethan's desk. "There. But he was careful. Obsessed with order. If something's missing... I'll know."

They moved together without speaking, old instincts resurfacing—like two people who'd once learned to navigate a shared storm. She sifted through journals slowly, her fingertips brushing the covers as though they might bruise under too much pressure. Jacob took out his phone, opened the camera app, and began photographing Ethan's notes.

"Do you know what this is?" he asked, pointing at a coded phrase scribbled in the margin of one notebook:

"Opus Gate. E42. Confirmed for Sofia. Ankara uncertain."

"No," Hannah murmured. "But that handwriting—it's recent. He was tense the last time he wrote in that one. Kept reaching for it even when we were out for dinner."

Jacob's jaw tightened. "This isn't just corporate politics. 'Opus Gate' sounds like a codename—something he'd only jot down if encryption wasn't available."

They continued searching. Hannah lifted a folded scarf from the bottom drawer and paused. Beneath it, taped to the wood, was a flash drive.

Jacob let out a soft whistle. "Now that... looks promising."

Just then, Hannah turned toward the window.

"What is it?" he asked.

"I thought I saw someone outside... just standing by the lamppost. Watching."

Jacob moved quickly, careful not to disturb the curtains as he peeked through. The street was empty now—only a dog sniffing near the curb and a woman pushing a stroller uphill.

"No one there now."

But the air shifted. And so did they.

Jacob set the flash drive on the desk like it might bite him.

"Let's not plug it in just yet," he muttered, reaching into his satchel for a portable external scanner. "Last thing we need is malware or a tracker pinging whoever gave Ethan this."

Hannah hovered nearby, arms crossed, hands curled tight under her elbows. She didn't realize she was swaying slightly until she caught her own reflection in the dark monitor. Her face looked pale, lips slightly parted, like she'd been holding her breath since last night.

Jacob connected the scanner to his laptop and inserted the drive into it instead.

"You always travel with gear like this?" she asked, voice thin but curious.

He gave a half-smile. "Paranoia makes a good companion in my line of work."

The scan ran. No threats detected.

He finally slid the drive into his laptop, then activated a discreet AI interface he'd been using for the past year.

"All right, Hem. Keep watch," Jacob said under his breath.

A calm male voice—precise, clipped, British—responded from the machine:

> "Monitoring active. Let me know if you require decryption or metadata assessment."

Hannah blinked. "Hem?"

"Short for Hemingway. I figured if I was going to argue with an AI, it might as well be with someone who knows how to write."

Despite herself, she smiled.

The screen loaded slowly. One folder appeared: DELTA_43_ANK-SOF

"Ankara to Sofia," Jacob said, narrowing his eyes. "This might be a timeline. Or an extraction route."

Inside were four files:

- A spreadsheet named "D-Logs_Sessions"
- A scanned document: "Client K – Redacted.pdf"
- A small audio file: "11_20_clear.mp3"
- And a video titled: "NIX_BLACK.mp4"

"Start with the video," Hannah said, wrapping her arms tighter across her chest.

Jacob gave a nod and double-clicked.

The screen flickered, struggling under the poor resolution. A dim office appeared—cold lighting, shadowed corners, like a surveillance cam from the mid-2000s. Ethan's voice came through first, muffled but urgent.

"If you're seeing this, it means I didn't make it to Sofia. Ankara is compromised. David's not who he says he is. Watch the accounts. Watch Kaplan."

Then static.

Then another voice followed, filtered and artificial—digitally masked.

"Terminate. No loose ends. Use Kaplan if necessary."

The video ended.

Hannah stepped back slightly, breath caught somewhere between her chest and throat. "He knew," she whispered. "He knew they were coming for him."

Jacob sat still, fists clenched on the desk. He clicked on the spreadsheet. Dozens of rows, colour-coded with dollar figures, initials, and location markers.

One row made them freeze:

E.G. - $45,000 - 'clearance adjusted' - 22-OCT-2024

Hannah leaned forward. "That's Ethan. He never abbreviated—but that's his handwriting in the margin."

Jacob snapped a picture with his phone and fed the data into Hem.

"Cross-checking with local transit and customs activity between Ankara and Sofia," the AI intoned softly.

As they waited, Hannah glanced toward the window. Her breath caught.

"There," she said, nodding.

Across the street, a man stood beside a newspaper kiosk. He wasn't reading. Just standing—still, too still. Then, as if feeling her gaze, he turned and walked off without buying anything.

Jacob followed her eyes, but the man was gone.

"That wasn't a coincidence," she said.

"No," Jacob replied, already logging the time and description in Hem's system. "This is surveillance. And we just lit up on their radar."

A tension hung between them—not of conflict, but of clarity.

Ethan hadn't just stumbled onto something.

He had started a war.

And now, whether they liked it or not, they were on the front line.

Jacob backed up the contents of the flash drive to an encrypted vault and wiped the local session clean. Hem logged the operation silently.

"Whoever's watching us," Jacob said, "they're not amateurs. Which means we need to move. Fast."

He crossed to the window and drew the curtain halfway—enough to let light in, not enough to give anyone a clear view inside.

Hannah paced near the coffee table, phone in hand, but not dialing. Her thumb hovered over Ethan's number again and again, as though sheer will could force a reply. Her skin prickled with that invisible sensation—the one where you know eyes are on you.

"Do you think he left that flash drive for me to find?" she asked, her voice more fragile than she intended.

"I think he knew exactly how you'd respond. You're methodical, but you lead with your gut. That's why he trusted you to carry this if he couldn't."

She nodded, but her gaze remained distant.

Suddenly, Hem chimed in:

"Motion alert. Unknown Bluetooth signal attempting low-range sync with this system. Proximity within twenty meters."

Jacob's spine went rigid.

"That's not good."

He moved quickly to the balcony, scanning rooftops and parked vehicles. A black scooter idled across the street. No rider. No license plate.

"Istanbul scooters don't usually ghost idle," Jacob muttered.

A low click sounded from the hallway—something metallic. Not a knock.

Jacob turned to Hannah. "Get your passport. Just in case."

Hannah stared at him. "Now?"

"They know we've accessed the files. It's no longer just about Ethan—it's about damage control. We've got a ten-minute window, max."

She didn't argue. She moved fast.

Within minutes, she returned with her travel pouch and a tremble in her hands. "Where are we going?"

"Somewhere noisy. Somewhere with a crowd." Jacob glanced at the coffee table and grabbed the burner phone from his bag. "And somewhere no one expects us."

He tapped into Hem. "Lock system. Data dump to cloud. Erase local. Protocol Nine."

Hem replied:

"Confirmed, System purge in progress. You have five minutes."

They were out the door within three.

Istanbul breathed differently outside.

As Hannah and Jacob emerged into the streets of Bebek, the city's rhythm surrounded them like a living tide—impossible to ignore, too vast to grasp. The late afternoon air was brisk, laced with the scent of damp stone, sweet simit bread, and roasted chestnuts curling from carts near the sidewalk. Golden light caught on the domes and rooftops, bouncing off the distant glint of the Bosphorus.

Taxis honked with impatient zeal, weaving between cars like fish in a tightly packed school. The roads, predictably congested, buzzed with scooters darting around stalled buses. A man argued in rapid Turkish over a parking spot while two teenage girls sat cross-legged on a low stone wall nearby, sharing headphones and laughter.

Above them, Ottoman-stained alleyways branched off from the main street, cobbled and narrow, whispering old secrets with every footstep. People didn't just live in Istanbul—they survived it, danced with it, wrestled it daily. And somehow, it held them all.

"I've never gotten used to the pace," Hannah murmured.

Jacob smirked. "It's a city that keeps its secrets loud."

As they reached the corner of a busy junction, a little boy—no more than six—broke free from his mother's grip and darted into Hannah's path, nearly colliding with her.

"Afedersiniz!" he cried, looking up with wide, alarmed eyes.

Hannah instinctively steadied him with a hand on his shoulder. "It's okay," she whispered, her voice catching.

The mother rushed forward, breathless and embarrassed. "Çok özür dilerim, hanımefendi."

"No harm," Hannah replied, her Turkish soft but certain.

The boy cast one more glance at her before disappearing into the crowd.

Jacob said nothing, but something flickered in his expression—a silent acknowledgment of the moment. A reminder that in the middle of chaos, life went on.

—They turned a corner and vanished into the thrum of the city.

Chapter Four - Fragile Alliances

Karaköy was Istanbul in miniature—where history hummed beneath the cobblestones and modern commerce never slept.

Once known as Galata, this ancient port city had been a Genoese outpost, a center for European merchants, and a cultural hinge between East and West. Now, it buzzed with hip galleries, waterfront bistros, and men in suits talking crypto over Turkish tea. At the mouth of the Golden Horn, Karaköy breathed both memory and ambition.

It was also Cem Halman's turf.

The café—Gülhané—sat tucked between a stone-carved alley and a minimalist design store, its Ottoman tiles climbing halfway up the walls before giving way to industrial beams and Edison bulbs. The smell of fresh baklava floated just beneath the stronger aroma of dark-roasted coffee and grilled cheese börek.

"This is his place," Jacob said as they approached. "He's here most days. Knows the staff. Keeps his ears open."

Hannah hesitated, pulling her coat tighter. "You're sure he's reliable?"

"He's not. But he's useful."

Inside, Cem sat in his usual spot—corner table, back against the wall, rust-coloured jacket open like a statement. He sipped his tea with the boredom of someone used to danger arriving late.

Jacob led them over. "Cem."

"Jacob Adler," Cem said, smiling like a knife. "I thought you left town with your tail between your legs."

"And yet, here I am."

Cem's gaze flicked to Hannah. "The sister. The one who never needed saving. Welcome to my humble lair."

She said nothing, only slid into the booth beside Jacob.

Cem took another sip. "So, who's dead—or about to be?"

"Ethan," Jacob said plainly. "He vanished two nights ago."

Cem raised an eyebrow. "That explains the chatter."

"What chatter?" Hannah asked, sharp.

"Your husband's name hit a few filters. Port movements, private charters, chatter across the Black Sea corridor. Someone with reach is asking questions—and scrubbing others."

"You always had your ear in deep places," Jacob said carefully.

Cem shrugged. "You forget, I was once the middleman for men like Ethan. He was too clean for that world. But when clean men go missing, it sends ripples."

Jacob leaned in. "We need information—movement logs, calls, anything on Mehmet Orman. Ethan mentioned him."

Cem's eyes sharpened. "Kaplan's not a name you drop lightly. If your boy was brushing up against him, he was playing a game he didn't understand."

"Help us understand," Hannah said quietly.

"I can. But it costs."

Jacob nodded before she could protest. "We'll pay."

"No cash," Cem said, grinning. "A favor. Later."

He reached into his jacket and slid a folded slip of paper across the table.

"A private Orion-affiliated jet left Ankara the night Ethan vanished. It didn't land in Sofia—it went to Bucharest. Emre Kaplan was on it."

Hannah's voice was barely a whisper. "And Ethan?"

"If he was on that plane, he was either protected... or vanished on purpose."

Cem leaned in one final time. "One more thing. The moment you walked in here, you stopped being invisible. So finish your tea. And start moving."

The buzz of conversation in Gülhané Café faded behind them as Hannah and Jacob stepped out into the narrow street. But the warmth of the space did not follow. A breeze from the Bosphorus tugged at Hannah's coat, sharp and sudden, setting her nerves tingling all over again.

"Don't look behind you," Jacob murmured, already scanning the reflections in the darkened shop windows. "Right side, twenty meters back. Same guy from Bebek."

Hannah didn't respond, but she felt it—the scrape of unseen eyes down her spine.

"Did he follow us from the apartment?"

"Maybe. Or maybe he just picked us up here. Cem's tip-off might've flushed someone out of hiding."

The street was bustling: tourists posing near graffiti walls, street vendors calling out simit prices, teenagers filming TikToks in front of an old mural. But Jacob's tone had a new edge—tight, clipped. She recognized it from years ago, when he'd called her from a border crossing after a story went sideways in Beirut.

They turned into a narrower lane, passing a tattoo parlor and a quiet bakery, the scent of cardamom-laced bread softening the air. It should have felt safe. It didn't.

Hannah caught her reflection in a glass door—hazy and off-center. She almost didn't recognize herself. The scarf tucked around her neck, the tense set of her mouth, the narrowed gaze that scanned the street behind her. This wasn't the woman who spent hours at the Süleymaniye Library, poring over 15th-century Ottoman manuscripts, fingers smudged with ink, eyes lighting up at every deciphered annotation. Back then, she'd lose herself in time — not in fear.

She remembered Ethan visiting her at the archive once, leaning against the stone archway with coffee in hand and a smirk on his face. "You disappear into books the way I disappear into spreadsheets," he'd said. "Difference is, yours smell like parchment and revolution."

She'd laughed, heart full. He always saw her for who she was, even when she forgot.

Now... she wasn't sure who he was anymore. And that hollow truth echoed louder than the Istanbul traffic.

"Left," Jacob said, pulling her gently but urgently.

They ducked into a bookshop—narrow, ceiling-low, packed with volumes in Turkish, Arabic, English. Dust caught in the shafts of light. An old man behind the counter didn't look up from his tea.

Jacob moved to the back, pretending to browse. "Two options," he whispered. "We make for Kadıköy by ferry—blend in. Or we double back to the car and try to head for the highway."

Hannah didn't hesitate. "Ferry. You said it yourself—somewhere with a crowd."

Outside, the door creaked open.

Footsteps.

Jacob's shoulders tightened.

But it was only a tourist couple—loud, laughing, oblivious.

Still, the window for escape was closing.

Jacob tapped Hem's secure app on his burner phone. "Encrypting movement log. New destination: Kadıköy pier."

Hannah turned to him, eyes wide but calm.

"You okay?" he asked, finally meeting her gaze.

She nodded, then shook her head. "I don't know. I keep thinking... if he's really gone, what does that make the last seven years? What does that make me?"

Jacob exhaled slowly, voice low. "You're the person he trusted enough to leave a trail for. That has to mean something."

She looked at him then—not the brother she hadn't spoken to in years, not the disappointment her parents always whispered about. Just Jacob. Her brother. The one who used to walk her home from school in winter, shielding her from slush with his coat.

"I missed you," she said quietly.

Jacob blinked, surprised. "Yeah. Me too."

Then he pulled open the side door, and together they stepped back into the city's current—moving fast, with shadows close behind.

The ferry rocked gently as it pulled away from the dock, a low mechanical hum rising beneath the city's chorus of calls and horns. Hannah and Jacob stood at the rear deck, their backs to the thinning Karaköy skyline. Mist from the Bosphorus clung to their sleeves, and the wake behind them trailed like an unraveling thread.

"I used to love this part," Hannah murmured. "That feeling of slipping between continents. Like Istanbul was letting you go—just a little."

Jacob leaned on the rail beside her. "I always thought the water kept the city honest. Everything else changes... but this—this is still the same grey-blue chaos it's always been."

They didn't speak for a while. Around them, the deck buzzed softly with movement—students in headphones, commuters with tired eyes, a woman reading aloud from a children's book to a sleepy toddler. Normal life, unaware of the hunt in its midst.

Kadıköy was coming into view now, stretching out with its colorful streets and café-lined avenues. Once known as Chalcedon in antiquity—long before it became a vibrant hub on Istanbul's Asian side—it had been the site of great theological councils and Byzantine debates, a place where empires argued about gods. Now, it pulsed with modern spirit: graffiti, music, antique bookstores, and steaming cups of Turkish tea in tulip-shaped glasses.

Jacob watched the opposite shore grow clearer—"We won't be safe long," he said. "Once Cem's info hits the wrong ear, they'll widen the net."

Hannah nodded. Her fingers were cold around the ferry rail. "You think Ethan was trying to bring it down? Orion?"

"Maybe not the whole thing," Jacob said. "But a part of it. A powerful part."

A gull shrieked overhead, cutting through the quiet like a warning bell.

Hannah turned her face into the wind. "Do you remember that summer in Asbury Park? When you told Dad you wanted to be a journalist?"

Jacob smiled faintly. "And he said, 'Writers don't make money. They make enemies.'"

"He wasn't wrong."

"He also wasn't subtle."

They both laughed—quiet, fleeting.

"I should have written to you," Jacob said suddenly. "When everything went down with the exposé. When I left. I was ashamed. And angry. Mostly at myself."

Hannah didn't look at him. "I wanted to be angry at you forever. It was easier than admitting I missed you."

As the ferry slowed, Hannah watched the terminal buzz with the weekend crowd.

Tourists posed in front of the Bull Statue—a symbol of resistance turned selfie spot. A group of college students followed a food tour guide toward the famous Çiya Sofrası, already filming their next bite. Near the Moda shoreline, families unwrapped picnic lunches under the shade of old fig trees while musicians played melancholic rock with soft Greek undertones.

It was beautiful. And so terribly unaware.

Hannah straightened, suddenly sharp again. "Do we have a contact on this side?"

"Yeah. A fixer. Discreet. Speaks five languages, owes me two favors."

"Do I get to ask what you did for him?"

"No," Jacob said. "You really don't."

The ramp clanked open, and the crowd began to shift. The ferry had delivered them, but it hadn't left the danger behind.

As they stepped into the swell of bodies moving toward the Kadıköy terminal, neither looked back.

But both knew someone probably was.

"Do you think Ethan ever made it here?" she asked softly.

"If he did," Jacob said, "he wouldn't have come as Ethan."

—And just like that, Istanbul became a different kind of map.

Chapter Five - Into the Shadows

The Kadıköy backstreets were quieter now, the city humming low as if holding its breath.

Jacob led Hannah through a narrow alley where the walls closed in like secrets. They stopped before a rusted iron door tucked between a shuttered antique shop and a crumbling bookbinder. Over the door, a tile mosaic had partially survived the wear of decades — a single tulip motif, etched in cobalt and crimson, curled into the shape of a flame.

Hannah's gaze lingered on it. "Tulip," she whispered. "Lâle. It's from the Tulip Era—Lâle Devri."

Jacob looked up. "You'd know."

She ran a finger lightly over the cracked tile. "1718 to 1730. The Ottoman elite were obsessed with them. It was a period of beauty, indulgence... before rebellion brought it all crashing down."

Jacob's mouth twitched. "Fitting for this place."

This building, once part of an Ottoman scribe's guild hall, had been repurposed over and over—each reinvention hiding the previous one. Now it was Aydin Miroğlu's den. A place that remembered opulence but now survived on silence.

Jacob knocked—twice, pause, once more.

The door opened. Aydin looked like someone carved out of dried bark: lean, hollow-cheeked, eyes like flint under heavy brows.

"I said I don't work with ghosts," he growled.

"You did once," Jacob replied.

Aydin eyed Hannah. "She your conscience or your cover?"

"She's the reason I'm still in Istanbul."

A long pause. Then Aydin stepped aside. "Get in before the tulip fades."

Inside, the air was thick with dust, cologne, and secrets. The walls were lined with photographs, old radios, hand-sketched maps, and a corkboard overflowing with red-thread connections. Jacob paused, his eyes finding a newspaper clipping pinned to the side.

"Didn't think you kept that," he said quietly.

"Hard to forget the man who nearly got me disappeared in Sofia," Aydin replied dryly.

Hannah glanced between them. "You two go back?"

Jacob let out a breath. "He was a source. Then a partner. Then... I burned him."

"Left me in a basement with nothing but a dead comm link and a bowl of sour lentils," Aydin muttered. "But he also warned me just in time. So I guess we're even."

Hannah looked at her brother—really looked. "Is this who you became while we weren't speaking?"

Jacob met her gaze, unflinching. "Parts of me were always this. You just stopped looking."

A moment passed.

Then Aydin turned to his desk and picked up a flash drive. "Your ghost," he said to Jacob. "He landed in Ankara two days ago. Boarded a private Orion-affiliated jet under diplomatic exemption. Destination: Bucharest."

Hannah's breath caught. "Was he alone?"

"No," Aydin replied. "Mehmet Orman was with him. That tells you everything you need to know."

He handed Jacob the drive. "One-time decrypt. Burn after reading."

Jacob nodded, his jaw set.

Aydin's gaze shifted back to Hannah. "He left you a trail, you know. That man of yours. He was scared, yes—but methodical. Left pieces behind for someone who could see past the panic."

Hannah clutched the flash drive like it might dissolve. "Why me?"

Aydin shrugged. "Maybe because he knew you were the only one who'd still believe in him."

Aydin disappeared into the back room, and the silence he left behind pressed down like fog.

Hannah ran her thumb over the smooth plastic of the flash drive, brow furrowed. "Why did Ethan trust Mehmet? He was so careful with everyone else."

Jacob stared at the corkboard, eyes tracing lines that connected Ethan's name to faces neither of them recognized. He was quiet for a beat too long.

"He didn't trust Mehmet," Jacob said finally. "Not really."

Hannah turned to him.

"I didn't tell you before because I wasn't sure it mattered," Jacob continued. "But last year—months before any of this—Ethan contacted me."

Hannah's breath caught. "What?"

"He wanted advice on how to leak something anonymously. Big. Financial corruption tied to state contracts. He asked about secure channels, burner protocols. Said it wasn't for publication—just... insurance."

Her expression shifted—confusion, betrayal, understanding—all tangled in seconds.

"Why didn't you tell me?" she asked, stunned.

"Because I didn't want to believe it. And because I thought he was testing me."

Hannah looked shaken. "Testing you?"

Jacob's voice was low. "He said he needed to know if I was still willing to do the right thing... even if it meant becoming a target again. Even if it meant protecting you."

The silence that followed was vast.

Hannah's lips parted. She wanted to ask more, but couldn't yet find the words. Everything she thought she knew about her husband was starting to shift, like a mosaic coming undone—only to reveal something larger beneath.

Jacob broke the tension gently. "He trusted you, Han. But he counted on me too. I think that's what scares me most."

He glanced at the wall of maps and string. "He was trying to cover his bases. I think he knew this would come for him eventually."

The silence that followed wasn't cold. It was contemplative. Grief, drawn quietly.

The air outside Aydin's den was sharp with evening salt and streetlamp heat. The tulip tile above the rusted door glowed faintly gold, a quiet farewell from the building that had once housed scribes who preserved the empire's secrets. Now it was passing them a secret of its own.

It was just past 9:30 PM—the streets quieter, edgier. Hannah and Jacob moved quickly through the narrowing lanes of Yeldeğirmeni, one of Kadıköy's oldest quarters. The cracked facades of century-old apartment blocks leaned like elders, watching. Murals bloomed across weathered brick walls—faces of forgotten poets, pigeons in flight, hands reaching but never touching.

Beneath their feet, cobblestones mapped centuries of memory. Hannah couldn't help but think about how Ottoman messengers once used these very lanes, delivering handwritten imperial decrees. Now she and Jacob were carrying something just as dangerous—digital truths dressed as whispers.

Jacob's phone buzzed softly—a coded blink from Hem.

> "New ping: thermal anomaly, 2 blocks behind. Likely tail. Recommend alternate route."

"Hem's still got eyes," Jacob said, showing her the signal.

They doubled back, ducking down a steep set of stairs that led past a dimly lit tea house and an antique shop that still displayed Ottoman swords in its window. The trail led them down to the bustling coastal road and toward the Kadıköy Ferry Terminal—a place humming with history.

The terminal's arched ceilings, whitewashed and trimmed in navy blue, echoed faintly with the rhythm of foot traffic and engines humming on water. The building had stood since the early 20th century, a later echo of the Ottoman Empire's grand maritime ambitions. In those days, the Sultan's messengers would cross from Asia to Europe aboard imperial barges—heavily adorned, crewed by men in kaftans, diplomacy wrapped in ritual.

Now, the ferry was less adorned but no less symbolic. It was still a passage—a crossing between old and new, between hiding and fleeing.

They boarded the 10:00 PM ferry to Eminönü, with just enough time to catch the overnight Bosphorus Express, which would connect to the Bucharest-bound route at the Yedikule rail junction.

Hannah leaned on the railing as the boat pushed away from the dock. "Why not fly?" she asked quietly. "It would've been faster. Cleaner."

Jacob kept his voice low. "Flying's predictable. Limited security checks, yes—but all digital trails. The rail system's slower, messier. And every change of train gives us a chance to disappear."

She nodded, but her brow furrowed. "And what about Hem?"

"He'll run passive. No uplinks. Only local reads. If anything sniffs at us too closely—thermal, Bluetooth, compromised Wi-Fi—we'll know before they do."

The lights of Tophane Pier sparkled across the water, growing larger as the ferry drew closer to the European side. Ottoman warehouses lined the shoreline—now converted into modern art spaces and cafés, but still bearing the insignias of their past: tughra symbols, imperial seals etched in stone.

Hannah watched the waves churn below. "If we get caught before we get out…"

"We won't," Jacob said.

And this time, she believed him.

The ferry glided into the Eminönü dock like a whisper carried over centuries.

The Galata Bridge stretched in the distance, layered with car headlights and fishing lines. Above it, the spires of the Süleymaniye Mosque crowned the hill—its domes silvered under moonlight, its silhouette unchanged since the reign of Suleiman the Magnificent, the longest-reigning sultan of the Ottoman Empire. Known as Kanuni, or the Lawgiver, Suleiman's rule marked the empire's golden age, blending territorial expansion with judicial reform, art, and architecture. The mosque bearing his name was the masterwork of the great architect Mimar Sinan, built to overlook the Golden Horn like a guardian of legacy and power.

Even the air felt older here, scented with coal smoke, salt, and something sweet from the late-night chestnut vendor near the quay.

Hannah exhaled slowly as they stepped onto the dock.

The stone beneath her feet had welcomed pilgrims, merchants, spies. Now it welcomed fugitives with nothing but a flash drive and fading trust.

Jacob adjusted the strap of his messenger bag and scanned the dark edges of the square.

"Hem?"

A soft pulse blinked across his screen:

"All clear."

They didn't speak as they moved, weaving through the thinning crowd toward a waiting taxi, the massive shadow of Süleymaniye Mosque trailing behind them.

Tomorrow, the city would wake to seagulls and sirens.

Tonight, they disappeared—into the veins of a continent, chasing the ghost of a man they both loved in different ways.

And the story was only just beginning.

—He'd left something behind, She could feel it.

Chapter Six - Rail Lines and Ghost Trails

I t was nearly 10:45 pm when Hannah and Jacob stepped into the grand echoing halls of Sirkeci Station—a place where whispers from history mingled seamlessly with modern reality.

Built in 1890 as the eastern terminus of the famed Orient Express, Sirkeci was a marvel of its age. Designed by the German architect August Jachmund, the station's style merged Ottoman elegance with European flair, capturing Istanbul's essence as the gateway between two worlds. Through these arches, diplomats, spies, royalty, and adventurers had passed, their stories forever whispered into the mosaic tiles and towering stained-glass windows, whose colours still shimmered softly under modern lights.

Hannah paused to soak it all in, her gaze drawn upwards to the elaborate frescoes on the ceiling—patterns of vines and tulips swirling in delicate Ottoman symmetry. It struck her that this station, once central to stories of intrigue and romance, was about to become part of hers.

Around them, fellow passengers reflected the city's social tapestry—business travellers tapping distractedly at smartphones, their tailored suits and polished shoes suggesting after-work catch-ups or drinks; a young couple, backpacks bursting, discussing their itinerary with bright-eyed enthusiasm; elderly travellers wrapped in modest shawls, murmuring quiet conversations in

Turkish, perhaps visiting family far away. Each person, Hannah realised, was a fragment of Istanbul's complex mosaic.

A gentle chime signalled their platform, and they moved with quiet urgency toward the train. Sleek silver with a ribbon of navy trim, the train waited gracefully. Panoramic windows offered enticing glimpses into comfortable, warmly-lit interiors—a reassuring blend of efficiency and romance, like travelling within an elegant cocoon.

They found seats near the rear carriage. Jacob discreetly activated Hem, receiving an immediate subtle buzz:

> "Security scans active. No anomalies detected. Decoding initiated."

Jacob relaxed slightly. "Hem's up. We'll know if anyone's following."

Hannah nodded, settling into her seat. The conductor's whistle pierced softly through the air, and the train glided smoothly from the station.

Jacob glanced sideways at her. "You alright?"

She looked at him, lips curving faintly. "The last time I took a train from here, Ethan was with me."

Jacob nodded knowingly, giving her space to continue.

She hesitated, then smiled softly. "We'd argued the night before—something petty, the usual. But once we were onboard, everything softened. Ethan just leaned close and whispered, 'Funny how trains make us forget why we were angry.'" She shook her head gently. "He always saw trains as magic. Something about journeys and second chances."

Jacob stared quietly, absorbing her words.

Hannah glanced at him carefully. "Why did you really choose the train, Jake? Not just the logistics—why?"

Jacob looked thoughtfully out the window, watching city lights blur into shadows. "I suppose Ethan was right. Trains are honest places. You sit still, the world moves around you. You can't outrun memories—just face them."

The rhythmic thud of wheels on rails filled the quiet. Hannah watched her reflection flicker across darkened glass, memories returning softly.

In that silence, a deeper, older memory surfaced—one from when they were younger, still living in Short Hills. She remembered clearly: one winter evening, she had hidden in the attic, crying softly after another of their parents' bitter arguments. She had been no older than fourteen, Jacob seventeen, already restless, already carrying burdens far heavier than a teenager should.

Jacob had found her, sat quietly beside her, and placed a battered copy of The Count of Monte Cristo in her lap. "Books are trains too, you know," he'd whispered, nudging her shoulder gently. "Open them, and they take you somewhere else."

The thought made her throat tighten even now. She turned towards him softly. "Do you remember that night in the attic?"

Jacob blinked slowly, clearly surprised she did. "I remember."

"You always knew how to make things feel lighter, even when they weren't."

He sighed softly. "And then I left—and made everything heavier."

Hannah gently touched his sleeve. "We both did our fair share of that."

The train sped into the darkness, Istanbul receding quietly behind them. Ahead lay uncertainty, risk, even danger—but perhaps also, Hannah thought, redemption.

Jacob glanced ahead, thoughtful. "Hem's decoding something significant, Han. Whatever Ethan left, it's got roots that run deep."

She nodded. Whatever awaited them in Bucharest, at least now they were facing it together.

The train settled into a steady, hypnotic rhythm as it glided through the Turkish countryside. Outside, darkness blanketed the landscape, occasionally pierced by the distant lights of villages—brief flashes of life, appearing and disappearing like whispered secrets.

Jacob watched his phone intently. Hem's decoding icon pulsed softly, progress bars dancing quietly in the background. Hannah observed him quietly, the subtle tension in his shoulders reminding her how much he carried beneath his calm exterior.

Just past midnight, Hem's notification lit up Jacob's screen:

"Decoding complete. New files decrypted. Analysis suggests hidden itinerary and key contacts in Bucharest. Advise immediate review."

Jacob exhaled sharply, glancing at Hannah. "We've got something."

He tapped the screen. Two files appeared:

- "BCH-RO-Logistics.pdf"
- "BCH-RO-Contacts.txt"

He opened the second file first. A short list appeared—names, phone numbers, notes in Ethan's familiar shorthand. At the top was highlighted:

"Professor Nikola Markov - University of Bucharest. Ottoman & Balkan History specialist. TRUST."

Hannah's eyes widened slightly. "Nikola Markov. I know that name—he co-authored papers with Ethan. They worked together briefly last year, remotely."

Jacob's brow furrowed. "Another historian?"

"Not just a historian—an expert on Ottoman influence across Eastern Europe. Ethan admired his work. They had planned to meet at a conference, but Ethan had to cancel suddenly."

Jacob nodded, quickly memorising the number. "We should contact him once we're clear of surveillance. Hem, can you run background checks?"

"Already in progress", came Hem's swift reply.

Hannah leaned back, thoughtful. "So Ethan knew he might end up in Bucharest all along. He was laying foundations."

"Exactly," Jacob agreed. "Ethan wasn't just running—he was planning ahead. Whatever he was uncovering, he knew it went deeper than Orion Global."

Silence settled around them again, interrupted only by the soft murmur of sleeping passengers and the distant, rhythmic hum of wheels on rails.

After a moment, Hannah quietly excused herself, slipping from her seat and moving down the sleek, open carriage towards the restroom. Modern European trains like this one had an airy openness, with spacious seating, unobstructed views through large panoramic windows, and gently illuminated aisles that made moving between sections easy and quiet.

As Hannah returned to her seat, moving softly through the quiet rows of passengers, she caught sight of something that made her pause. A man sat several rows away, illuminated softly by the warm glow of a discreet reading lamp clipped to his tray table. He was absorbed in meticulous note-taking, his calm, scholarly air drawing her attention immediately.

The leather-bound notebook in his hands was worn yet elegant, its corners softened from repeated handling, pages filled with neat annotations and delicate sketches of maps. Embossed gold lettering on the notebook's cover gleamed faintly in the soft light: "University of Bucharest."

Her breath stilled. Ethan had kept a similar notebook, a cherished gift from a colleague he'd often spoken warmly about.

She lingered discreetly, observing more closely. The man, likely in his mid-fifties, wore silver-rimmed glasses perched thoughtfully on his nose, greying hair combed neatly back. His clothing—a well-tailored tweed jacket over a navy sweater—suggested quiet dignity and scholarly precision.

She leaned subtly closer, realising he was murmuring softly into a digital recorder. His words, quiet yet distinct, reached her clearly: "...patterns of Ottoman trade routes across the Balkans becoming increasingly apparent... Ethan was correct."

Hannah's pulse quickened. She straightened quickly, her thoughts racing, and hurried quietly back to Jacob.

Jacob looked up immediately as she slid back into her seat, noticing her changed expression. "You alright?"

She leaned close, whispering urgently. "There's a man a few rows down—he mentioned Ethan by name. And he's from the University of Bucharest."

Jacob's eyes narrowed instantly, alert and focused. "Did you catch his name?"

"No, but his notebook—" Her voice caught slightly. "Jacob, it's exactly like Ethan's. They knew each other. I'm sure of it."

Jacob rose calmly. "Stay here. I'll introduce myself carefully. We need to know who he is."

She grabbed his arm gently. "Be careful."

Jacob smiled faintly, reassuringly. "Always."

He moved quietly down the aisle, leaving Hannah behind, her mind tumbling through unanswered questions. Was this man friend or foe—a thread Ethan deliberately left behind, or a new danger hidden behind coincidence?

She closed her eyes briefly, feeling the rhythmic sway of the train, and murmured softly to herself, echoing Ethan's words from long ago, "Journeys remind us who we really are."

Now, more than ever, she hoped those words were true.

Jacob paused politely by the man's side, speaking softly. "Excuse me—are you Professor Markov?"

The older man lifted his head, mild surprise giving way to gentle curiosity. "Yes—Nikola Markov. How can I help you?"

Hannah felt a quiet wave of relief as Jacob indicated gently towards her. "I'm Jacob Adler, and that's Hannah Goldstein. Ethan is her husband."

Professor Markov's expression shifted quickly, understanding dawning immediately. He closed his notebook carefully. "Then you must realise you're in great danger. Ethan contacted me days ago—he indicated he might need urgent assistance. When he didn't follow up, I feared the worst."

Jacob nodded solemnly. "We know. Ethan is missing, and Orion is involved."

Professor Markov's eyes darkened in concern. He quickly scribbled a phone number onto a page from his notebook, discreetly handing it to Jacob. "This isn't the place. Call me as soon as you arrive in Bucharest. Trust no one—these shadows run deep."

Jacob pocketed the note carefully, exchanging a knowing glance with Hannah as he returned to their seats.

The train plunged forward into the night, leaving them with new allies, deeper mysteries, and an unspoken question about Ethan's true intentions.

The transfer from Sirkeci to Halkalı had been swift—just under forty minutes, the train gliding quietly past sleeping suburbs and industrial estates, until they arrived at the edge of the city's reach. From Halkalı, they boarded the overnight regional train bound for Edirne, its carriages less polished than the one before but quieter, almost reverent in their silence.

By the time the first light crept over the Thracian hills, Hannah stirred slightly in her seat. The city of Edirne shimmered faintly into view—its silhouette marked by gentle domes and pointed minarets rising from behind a rolling bank of mist.

Edirne had once been the jewel of the Ottoman Empire—the capital before Istanbul, a city of sultans and scholars, the site of battles, alliances, and grand declarations. Its mosques and stone bridges whispered of power once absolute. Even half-asleep, the place radiated a quiet gravity.

They stepped off the train into cool, crisp air. The station was quiet, a few porters gathered near the doors, their breath visible in the morning chill. A handful of travellers dragged overnight bags toward waiting taxis, but no one paid Hannah and Jacob much notice.

"We've got a thirty-minute window before the next connection," Jacob murmured. "Plenty of time to disappear into someone else."

They found the traveller's lounge near the far platform—a quiet corridor with outdated sofas and clean, tiled washrooms. Jacob handed Hannah a change of clothes from his backpack, then vanished briefly into the men's side.

In the mirror of the women's washroom, Hannah studied herself—hair tousled, eyes shadowed by fatigue. She changed quickly into black jeans, a deep grey turtleneck, and a dark forest green utility jacket with a foldable hood. She tied her hair up into a high bun and wrapped a dark scarf loosely around her neck.

She didn't just look different. She felt it too—less like the grieving woman who had stood paralysed in their Istanbul flat, and more like someone who was learning to run toward answers rather than away from fear.

In the men's lounge, Jacob zipped up a casual navy hoodie over a white t-shirt and pulled on a beanie. His coat had a neutral cut, less structured, less traceable. He splashed cold water on his face, then stared into the mirror longer than necessary. His eyes were bloodshot but alert.

"Incoming: Surveillance sync alert. Partial match pinged. Low confidence score."

Hem's message blinked on his screen, no louder than a whisper. Jacob tapped to encrypt the data and cleared the feed. "They're looking. Not sure who, but someone's watching facial logs."

Outside, they regrouped beneath the overhang of the station arch. The Selimiye Mosque loomed faintly in the distance, its slender minarets piercing the pale blue sky. Mimar Sinan's masterwork—perhaps the most beautiful mosque in the empire's twilight. Ethan would've appreciated the irony: fleeing the shadows of a fallen empire under the gaze of its golden pinnacle.

"Do you remember that guide Ethan loved quoting?" Hannah asked softly, adjusting her scarf. "He called the Selimiye the crown on Sinan's soul."

Jacob smiled faintly. "He used to say that about you, too."

She looked at him, surprised. "He did?"

Jacob nodded. "He admired the way you studied things—how you made them beautiful just by understanding them."

A quiet silence settled between them.

"I never told him," Jacob added. "How much I respected him. How I envied what you two had."

Hannah's voice cracked just slightly. "He left notes. Breadcrumbs. In my books. In margins. Always clues. Half of what I know about him was hidden in underlines."

They stood side by side, watching the city stir slowly to life. A bus rumbled by. Somewhere, a shopkeeper rolled up his shutter. The moment felt still, suspended—fragile, but healing.

Jacob checked the time. "Train leaves in fifteen."

"Let's go," Hannah said, tugging her hood up. "We're not done chasing ghosts."

They began walking slowly, the station unfolding around them like a map they'd only just learned to read. The morning light sharpened edges, casting long shadows across the cobblestones. Each step felt quieter than the last, but not from fear anymore—something else was settling in.

Resolve.

Hannah glanced sideways at her brother. He wasn't the boy who had disappeared from their family all those years ago. Nor was she the woman Ethan had left behind in Istanbul. Something was shifting between them, quiet and tentative. Not forgiveness, perhaps—but understanding. And that was enough for now.

She touched the folded paper in her pocket—the decrypted notes from Hem, the name Professor Markov underlined twice by Ethan's hand.

He planned for this, she thought. He trusted us to follow.

Jacob tilted his head as if sensing her thought. "Do you think he's still alive?"

"I have to," she whispered. "Otherwise... none of this would make sense."

The train's distant horn echoed across the platform.

They didn't run. They walked toward the sound, side by side, shadows lengthening behind them, while the past—complicated, aching, unfinished—followed a step behind.

—Someone's watching the watchers.

Chapter Seven - Into the Fold (Bucharest Arrival)

The full journey from Istanbul to Bucharest had taken them across borders and time zones. From Sirkeci, they rode west to Halkalı, then continued overnight through Edirne, Kapıkule, Svilengrad, and Ruse, before finally crossing into Romania in the early evening. Each stop was brief but grounding with breaks long enough to mark invisible borders and customs officials too tired to care much beyond passports and a passing glance – a reminder of how far they'd come, and how much still lay ahead.

Sometime between the rolling hills of Bulgaria and the flat sprawl of southern Romania, the tension eased just enough for rest. They had taken turns sleeping—Hannah first, curled into the window seat, Jacob watching the corridor, alert even in stillness. Then he drifted off as Hem continued quietly decoding in the background.

The hum of the rails lulled Hannah into dreams not of danger, but memory.

Ethan sat beside her at their kitchen table in Short Hills, hair mussed, eyes soft. He was writing something—always writing—and when she reached for her cup, he smiled faintly without looking up. "It's never about the door, Han," he said quietly. "It's about the pattern on the frame."

She stirred in her sleep, the phrase lingering, curling around a part of her mind like a wisp of smoke.

When she woke, the train was pulling through the outskirts of Bucharest, the sun is cresting the horizon, casting long golden streaks across battered apartment blocks and factories that hadn't changed since the Cold War. The skyline was a clash of eras—cranes perched beside crumbling Orthodox domes, concrete towers softened by vines.

"It's 6:40," Jacob said, tapping his phone. "Warkov said 7:00. Café Opal—across from the station."

Hannah blinked, still half in her dream. "The one with the mint tea?"

They hadn't seen Professor Warkov again after the first leg of the journey. He had quietly slipped away at the transfer in Halkalı, later arriving in Bucharest by flight. But before departing, he'd slipped a folded note into Jacob's jacket—time, location, and a quiet instruction: "Ask for mint tea."

The train exhaled into Gara de Nord, its brakes grinding like tired lungs. As they stepped on the platform, the city hit them—smoky, cold, alive with quiet energy.

Gara de Nord was a monument of history layered upon itself. Built in the late 1800s to welcome kings and foreign emissaries, then repurposed under communist rule, and now standing as both gateway and graveyard of stories. Arches strained under age, neon signs flickered above weary kiosks, and locals moved quickly, heads down, like people accustomed to being watched.

Hem sent a soft notification to Jacob's burner:

"Surveillance low. Thermal trace detected two hours ago at station café entrance. Confidence: 29%. Possible pre-flagged location. Proceed."

They exited quickly, blending with the tide of commuters. Across the boulevard, the café stood beneath a rusted cinema marquee—Café Opal, its windows warm, fogged slightly from inside. A place that didn't ask questions. A place that smelled like cloves and paper and conversations meant only to be half-heard.

The café was called Hanul Timpului—The Inn of Time.

It was the kind of place that seemed to listen more than speak. Once a 19th-century Han (means Inn in Romania), a caravanserai where travellers from across the Balkans sought rest and warmth, it had been rebuilt, repurposed, and reimagined across regimes. Ottoman traders had once dined beneath its wooden beams. In the interwar years, poets and revolutionaries debated politics over black coffee and plum brandy. Then came war, then silence, then a quiet rebirth in the hands of artists and writers who turned its upstairs rooms into studios and its ground floor into what it was now—a café with its heart still listening. The air smelled of citrus polish, old wood, and mint leaves warming slowly in porcelain.

Outside, the morning unspooled slowly. The light over Bucharest was sharp and metallic, streaking through gaps in the tram cables above the street. The cafés and kiosks on the boulevard blinked to life one by one, shutters rising, coffee machines hissing, early city dwellers murmuring into phones or ducking into coats. It was a city stretching its limbs after a long, cautious sleep.

Inside Hanul Timpului, time itself seemed to pause. The wooden tables were scuffed but clean, each bearing a different burnished candleholder, flickering low even in daylight. Walls lined with sepia-toned photographs gave silent nods to past patrons long gone. And three people threading the needle of memory and fear.

Professor Nikola Markov rose gently from the cornet booth beneath an old painting of the Carpathians as Hannah and Jacob approached him, offering Hannah the kind of nod reserved for grieving families at closed-casket funerals. Jacob slid into the seat across from him, placing his bag within arm's reach. Hannah followed, eyes locked on the professor.

"Why Bucharest? "Why now?"" Hannah asked, her voice brittle but steady.

Professor Markov poured tea without speaking for a moment, the silence not uncomfortable, but weighted. When he looked up, his gaze was fixed, deliberate.

"Because this is where Ethan's trail stopped," Warkov replied, "At least officially."

Pouring the tea with precision, his hands not shaking, but not quite still.

Her breath caught at the name. She hadn't heard it spoken in days. Spoken by someone else.

"He came to me four weeks ago," Markov continued. "He looked... different. Like a man holding something too big in his chest." Said he'd uncovered something inside Orion's Eastern operations—something buried, encrypted, old. He was cautious, sharper than I'd ever seen him."

He paused, as if choosing his next words with surgical precision.

Jacob shifted slightly, not out of restlessness, but discomfort—wary of the weight Markov's words were already carrying.

"He asked me for access to an archive. Interwar records. Government contracts, political shadows, things not listed anywhere you could search online. Especially the 1930s and early '40s. He was looking for connections between shell corporations, cultural councils, and paramilitary groups that supposedly dissolved after the war. He was convinced that Orion Global was just a shell—part of something older, deeper. He called it *The Fold*."

Jacob frowned. "So it's not just a codename. It's a network?"

Markov nodded slowly. "An echo of Cold War diplomacy gone rogue. It's older than Orion. Older than any of the companies involved now. Think Cold War, pre-Warsaw Pact, covert cooperation between nationalist groups. It existed in the cracks—across Romania, Bulgaria, Moldova, Turkey, even further east. Ethan believed it never died. Only... adapted."

Markov lowered his voice.

"He mentioned the Iron Guard, Romania's ultra-nationalist militia. And a man named Tudor Radulescu, who vanished from public record in 1941 but had financial links to Balkan trade routes still active under different names."

Hannah blinked. "And he thought these... ghosts were connected to Orion?"

Markov nodded. "Orion is a mask, he said. The Fold has worn many."

He pulled a page from his notebook, sliding it across to Jacob: a list of names, dates, and cryptic notations.

● T. Radulescu – missing 1941 – reappears 1948 (code: Cedrela)

● I.G. Cultural Foundation – dissolved 1938 – assets absorbed into Balkan Mercantile Holdings (BMH)

● BMH subsidiary: Orion Istanbul Division

"These weren't just old names," Markov added. "They were passed down. Ownerships shifted. But the core remained the same.

"Hannah reached slowly for the tea, but didn't drink. Her fingers simply curled around the warmth like it was the only steady thing in the room.

Markov's gaze softened as he looked at her. "He mentioned you, you know. Not often. But when he did, it was always like he was borrowing strength."

Her throat tightened.

"He was private," she said quietly, "but not secretive."

Markov didn't challenge her. "Maybe he didn't want to burden you. Or maybe he didn't know how much danger he was in."

He slid a flash drive across the table. Then, slower, a folded piece of paper.

"Said I should only pass these on if he failed to check in."

Jacob reached for the flash drive, nodding. Hem would scan it later. For now, it sat between them like an unopened letter from the dead.

Hannah unfolded the note with both hands—carefully, with the reverance fo touch. Ethan's handwriting slanted across the page.

"If they find me first, don't follow my trail. Rebuild it. And start with the doorframe."

Her stomach dropped. The line from her dream. The kitchen. The ghost of Ethan murmuring while stirring his coffee.

"It's never about the door, Han. It's about the pattern on the frame."

Jacob saw it hit her. The colour draining, then returning. That flash of grief and wonder stitched together.

"You with me?" he asked gently.

She swallowed, blinked once, and nodded.

"He's still guiding us."

A silence settled between them, not awkward, but reverent.

Jacob looked at Markov. "Is there anyone else who knows what he was working on?"

Warkov hesitated, then shook his head.

"If there is, they've either disappeared... or they're part of what he was running from."

Outside, the sky had turned a pewter grey. The day had arrived. But inside, it still felt like dawn—where everything is fragile, and just beginning.

Hannah stared at Ethan's handwriting, her fingers trembling slightly, not from fear—but weight.

Every letter, every stroke was a whisper from him. Not dramatic. Not desperate. Just him, being deliberate, even in absence.

Start with the doorframe.

She read it again. Not metaphor. Not mystery.

Direction.

"Ethan wasn't being poetic," she said quietly, fingers brushing the paper like it was a relic. "He meant it literally. A physical doorframe. Ottoman. Patterned. Intentional."

Jacob tilted his head, trying to catch up. "Go on."

She leaned forward, her eyes clearing like glass wiped clean. "In Ottoman architecture, doorframes weren't just structural—they were symbolic thresholds. There's a whole philosophy around it: eşik bilgisi. Threshold knowledge. You pass under something sacred or secret, and you're changed by it. The symbolism was encoded in geometry—repeating tulips, eight-pointed stars, Kufic inscriptions hidden in linework."

Jacob nodded slowly. "Like passing into a different world."

"Exactly. But Ethan used to say some of these weren't just spiritual. They were communicative. Clues left in plain sight." She paused, the memory forming clearer now. "We studied one together. Years ago. A merchant house in Lipscani—the old Ottoman quarter. The frame had an unusual tulip motif. Ethan believed it wasn't ornamental. He said it reminded him of encryption glyphs."

Jacob's voice was soft now. "You think he's pointing you back to that house?"

"I know he is."

She sat back for a moment, caught between the now and the then.

A memory bloomed.

FLASHBACK

Ethan, kneeling before the frame, fingers tracing the carving, eyes bright with that unique thrill he reserved for hidden things. "The Ottomans buried meaning everywhere," he'd whispered. "But the best-kept secrets? They weren't on maps. They were in thresholds."

Jacob exhaled slowly. "This just turned from theory to map."

Hem buzzed once in Jacob's ear.

"Ottoman motif match confirmed. Lipscani district. Residence 19D. Unregistered ownership. Coordinates attached."

Jacob raised an eyebrow. "Hem's listening."

Hannah gave the slightest smirk. "Hem is always listening."

As they stood to leave, Professor Markov remained seated, watching them with a look that bordered on sadness. "Be careful in Lipscani," he said. "The past doesn't sleep well there."

Outside, the city had shrugged off dawn's fog. The hum of trolleys, the murmur of café chatter, the scent of roasted corn and exhaust blending into something distinctly Bucharest.

But as they stepped into the street, the world felt paused again—just for a second. That hush before truth begins to speak.

But beneath the cobblestones, something old stirred.

And the doorframe was waiting.

—Jacob looked back once toward the sealed chamber—toward the tulip, the scent, the fear in Ethan's unfinished warning.

Chapter Eight - The Pattern on the Frame

The Lipscani District was older than memory, older even than maps. Once the bustling core of Ottoman-era Bucharest, it had been home to silk traders, goldsmiths, and guild masters whose surnames still clung to fading street signs. Time hadn't passed through Lipscani — it had settled into its bones.

Its crooked lanes bore the weight of centuries: uneven cobblestones that had carried Ottoman hooves, communist boots, and now tourists in leather-soled shoes. Some buildings wore their restorations like proud new coats; others sagged, untouched, like ghosts too tired to beg for attention.

Café Hanul Timpului was just under 2.5 kilometres from the heart of Lipscani. Hannah and Jacob didn't risk a direct route. Hem flagged a thermal signature trailing two blocks behind them minutes after they left.

"There," Jacob muttered. He tilted his head slightly to the right, just enough for Hannah to catch the reflection in the dusty window of a passing tram. A figure, tall, coat unbuttoned, head slightly bowed—not close, but there. "Same one from the café. Can't confirm gender. Always keeping distance."

They veered off the main road, ducked into a narrow passageway flanked by old bookshops and a shoemaker's stall. Hannah followed without hesitation. Her scarf was drawn tight across her jaw; her posture straightened. She no longer walked like a woman reacting—she walked like someone preparing.

They slipped onto a local tram, then exited three stops later, weaving through a second-hand bookstore whose interior smelled of binding glue and lost lives. By the time they reached Lipscani, they had managed to lose the shadow figure—at least for now. Hem confirmed zero pings in the last six minutes.

"Doorframe's ahead," Hannah said quietly.

Jacob stopped her just before they turned the final corner. He pressed his back against the wall of a crumbling pharmacy and requested Hem for a survelliance, Hem pinged immediately;

"Surveillance sweep initiated... No trailing signals. Optical feeds within safe parameters. Proceed."

He gave her a short nod. "We're clean. Let's keep it that way."

They stepped around the corner—and there it was.

19D Lipscani stood quietly, like it had been waiting.

Wedged between a meticulously restored apothecary and a boarded-up printing press, the building bore its age like honour. The façade was washed in ochre that had long since lost its shine. Two small balconies jutted from above with curled iron railings, their floral motifs tangled with rust. The windows, arched and thin, were shadowed by wooden shutters sun-bleached to pale grey.

But the doorframe... the doorframe held everything.

Tulip carvings in interlocking loops crowned the entrance. The pattern wasn't decorative. It repeated with deliberate variance—each tulip slightly altered, layered like cipher glyphs. Hannah stepped closer, her breath caught.

"This is it," she whispered, brushing her fingers near the carving without touching. "It's the same pattern Ethan described."

Jacob looked upward, tracing the layout. The house was two floors, likely with a narrow attic and a shallow cellar based on Ottoman layouts. The upper floor was slightly recessed, typical of 17th-century merchant houses—providing shade and privacy. He recognised the ventilation slits beneath the window sills: originally for drying spices or silks, depending on the season.

"Locked," Jacob said after checking the handle. "Solid brass. Reinforced."

"No camera. No lights. No buzzer," he added, scanning around.

"We're not walking away," Hannah said, her jaw set.

They circled into the side alley, a narrow stretch littered with leaves and long-forgotten junk. A rusted gate hung open to one side, revealing a winding staircase that snaked up the rear.

Jacob looked at her. "We're not breaking in."

She arched a brow. "We're interpreting historical artefacts."

He almost smiled. "Fair enough."

They climbed carefully, Jacob leading. At the top, a small wooden door stood ajar. Hannah stepped through first, her breath catching at the scent: dust, age, something faintly acidic, like time itself.

Inside was shadow and silence.

A long corridor stretched forward, tiled in cracked mosaics—faint outlines of tulips and vines once vibrant with paint now dulled by soot. The walls held flaked plaster in warm tones, and remnants of deep walnut beams framed the ceiling.

This place had once been alive.

Hem buzzed.

"Architecture scan complete. Symbol match detected on interior lintel. Unknown cavity behind wall."

Jacob moved forward, hand against the wall. Hollow.

He used a folding tool to nudge the panel. It gave with a soft click.

Behind it: a sealed envelope, an aged calling card, and a fragment of an old Ottoman trade map—annotated in Ethan's distinct hand.

Jacob whistled. "He really did leave a trail."

Hannah lifted the envelope. On the back, in Ethan's all-caps script:

Only if she finds it.

They didn't speak. The silence was too heavy to carry with words.

Outside, the city muttered on—trams humming, coffee brewing, footsteps echoing in alleys.

Inside, the air held its breath.

The doorframe had spoken. And it was only the beginning.

Inside the hidden cavity, the envelope felt heavier than paper ought to. It was sealed with an aged wax stamp, cracked faintly at the edges but still intact — the impression? A tulip.

No initials. No crest. Just the tulip — stylised, sharp, Ottoman.

Hannah opened it with care, unfolding the letter inside. The paper was soft with age, but new enough to carry the scent of Ethan's cologne — the sandalwood and citrus blend she had once teased him for wearing like armour. Her eyes scanned the letter as Jacob leaned closer.

There weren't many words. Just coordinates. A date. And a line.

"If you've made it here, you're already part of the next layer."

She read it aloud. Her voice didn't tremble this time — it tightened.

Jacob took the paper and checked the coordinates using Hem. He turned the screen to her.

Location: Chişinău, Moldova

Marked Date: Four days from now

"A meeting?" Jacob asked.

"Maybe," Hannah replied. "Or a handoff."

The calling card was next. Jacob held it up. No name, just an embossed sigil — three interlocking circles, minimalist but striking. And one word beneath:

"Cedrela"

Hannah frowned. "Cedrela...?"

"Latin. It's a genus of trees," Jacob said. "Used to build stringed instruments... and coffins."

Hannah's eyes didn't leave the card. "Ethan used to say every cipher has a musical key."

Hem chimed again.

> "Cedrela: Codename linked to interwar Romanian network. See also: T. Radulescu. Ties to Balkan Mercantile Holdings."

Jacob's jaw tensed. "The same name Professor Markov mentioned. It's all feeding back into The Fold."

Then another alert from Hem.

"Proximity ping: Suspicious trace detected — 17 metres, low mobility, ground level."

Jacob was up instantly. He stepped carefully to the side window on the upper floor, reached for the monocular scope in his jacket

— no digital signals, no camera, just an old-fashioned lens — and scanned the street.

There. Across the road, half-obscured by a newsstand and a cracked lamppost, the figure stood watching. Still. Focused.

Jacob focused the monocular just long enough to catch a side profile — sharp jawline, dark stubble, high collar, dark beanie. A flick of a lighter.

He tapped a capture button built into the monocular's lens ring. A small, silent click.

"Image logged." appeared on the lens.

Back in his coat pocket, Hem blinked once.

"Snapshot uploaded to offline cache. Facial match algorithm initiated."

"Cross-referencing against encrypted profile set from Ethan's archive."

Jacob didn't linger.

"We've got a problem," he whispered. "Let's move."

Hannah didn't speak. She folded the map and card into the lining of her jacket, then wiped the dust from the shelf where the cache had been hidden.

"Fast. Quiet. No trace."

They worked in practiced silence. Jacob resealed the cavity and reset the panel. Hannah pocketed the wax seal and envelope. No fingerprints. No trail.

They exited out the back, looping through the alley, through a courtyard that smelled of damp stone and cooking oil, before emerging into a quiet cross street. Neither spoke as they merged with a slow-moving stream of early pedestrians — a delivery man, a pair of students, a vendor wheeling crates of oranges.

Three turns. Two misdirections. They didn't run. They vanished.

Hem buzzed.

> "Flag alert: Passport scan match – Ethan Goldstein. Chişinău Border Checkpoint. Time-stamped: 36 hours ago."

Jacob's heart kicked. He turned toward Hannah, who was watching traffic. He didn't need to say it.

She felt it.

Ethan was alive.

They crossed the boulevard and stepped into a tram heading west — neither looking back, neither letting hope shake their balance.

Another ping arrived from Hem — silent, deliberate.

> "Facial match complete. Subject: Milan Oruc. Orion Syndicate – Tactical Surveillance Unit. Last confirmed operation: Istanbul."

Jacob turned to Hannah, his voice quiet but firm. "It was him. The man watching the house. Milan Oruc. Orion's field team."

Hannah's expression barely shifted, but her eyes sharpened, locked in. No panic. Just calculation.

"So," she said evenly, "we're officially not alone."

Jacob looked away, eyes scanning the passing streets through the tram's weathered glass.

The man watching them... wasn't just observing.

He was assigned.

Jacob nodded once. "We're not just following Ethan's path anymore. We're walking in his shadow."

The tram carried them forward — quiet, steady — as the next city called them onward.

The sun had shifted overhead by the time Hannah and Jacob emerged from Lipscani. It was early afternoon in Bucharest, and the city's pulse had changed with it. Sidewalks were alive with motion—office workers in shirtsleeves and sunglasses, café tables brimming with laughter, cigarette smoke curling into crisp air. From Calea Victoriei, the heart of Bucharest's commercial core, came the scent of grilled meat, hot bread, and sugary pastries warming behind glass.

They moved calmly but deliberately, weaving through lunch crowds, letting the chaos of the noon rush become their cover. Hem sent soft pings of guidance, rerouting them away from flagged Wi-Fi zones and data clusters.

"Blend in. Move slow," Jacob murmured.

They paused at a corner where a vendor sold fresh mici—skinless sausages grilled until caramelized—served with mustard and a torn chunk of bread. Hannah and Jacob ate standing up, back to the crowd, like half the city around them.

They weren't strict observers of kosher dietary laws. Not anymore. That part of their upbringing had softened with time, practicality, and a thousand compromises since leaving home. The flavours were smoky, peppered with cumin and memory.

"Remember that hike after Mum died?" Jacob said suddenly.

Hannah looked up. "The one near the pine trail? When you wouldn't let me wander off?"

He smiled faintly. "You wandered anyway."

"I was chasing a fox."

"You got lost."

"I had a map."

He didn't say anything right away, then: "I promised Dad I'd never let you stay lost."

Hannah's gaze held his. "And I always knew you'd find me."

Bucharest drifted into mid afternoon with the calm of a city holding its breath. The lunch crowd faded to the shuffle of briefcases and newspaper vendors. Steam hissed from beneath a food cart as the scent of mici lingered in the air, thick with garlic and char.

Hannah and Jacob turned the corner near Calea Griviței, shoes clicking on the uneven sidewalk. Their bellies were full, their nerves not. The 7:10 p.m. Prietenia train to Chişinău was their plan. Slow. Overnight. Obscured. A pause in the chase — or so they thought.

Gara de Nord rose in front of them like a memory etched in iron and stone. Its canopy reached out like arms worn thin by history. The station had seen everything — kings, communists, liberation, and loss.

As they passed through the shadow of the outer archway, Hannah slowed, eyes tracing a series of chipped bas-reliefs near the columns.

"You know," she said, her voice quiet but charged, "this city used to be the hinge of an empire."

Jacob arched an eyebrow. He was used to her sudden dives into time.

"The Ottomans?" he asked.

Hannah nodded, stepping into the cool belly of the station, her gaze flicking between the mosaic-tiled floors and carved lintels.

"Wallachia and Moldavia were never fully conquered... but they were controlled. Vassal states. Ottoman suzerainty. It wasn't direct rule — it was subtler. Economic tributary. Political manipulation. Cultural absorption."

She gestured upward at a ceiling rosette edged in a near-Islamic floral pattern. "Some of these design motifs influenced by Ottoman artisans who passed through in the 18th century. You see it in the arches. The mosaic geometry. Even the spacing of public corridors — wide, formal, meant to command."

Jacob took it in, silent.

Hannah continued. "In 1396, the Battle of Nicopolis — Christian forces tried to push back, but failed. Then again at Varna in 1444. More blood. More empire."

Her tone darkened. "Vlad the Impaler came after that. He terrified the Ottomans. Guerrilla warfare. Forest ambushes. He ruled with cruelty, but he forced the empire to pause. That fear left marks in policy, border shifts... even architecture. Ottomans respected terror."

Jacob gave a soft whistle. "And now we're standing in a station that came just after the Treaty of Adrianople. 1829 — when Romania began shaking off the last Ottoman threads."

Hannah's eyes settled on a cracked window pane where light cut through like an old scar. "The influence never left. It's in the food, the land laws, even the way people build walls. It's all still here. Just dressed differently."

A moment of quiet fell between them — not the silence of tension, but of weight.

Then — *ping*.

Jacob flinched almost imperceptibly. It wasn't his phone.

A faint glint flickered on the edge of his glasses — a barely visible projection pulsed across the inner lens.

This was the first time Hannah noticed the detail — the shape of his frames had always seemed slightly bulkier than necessary. Now she understood. Hem was communicating directly through Jacob's smart glasses, discreet, real-time, hands-free.

"What is it?" she asked, voice low.

Jacob's eyes didn't move from the concourse ahead. "Orion contact. Lower platform. Facial match confirmed."

Hannah's breath slowed.

"Train?"

"Burned. Hem says risk's escalated. Too many eyes." A pause. "Flight's clean. Private terminal. Alias uploaded. We're rerouted."

Hannah turned from the ticket counter, heart thudding low in her chest. She took in the columns, the carved arches, the layered languages in the announcements. Ottoman lines blurred into Soviet ones. Old empires bled into modern surveillance.

She glanced at Jacob — at the tilt of his shoulders, how easily he'd pivoted course without panic.

And in that moment, memory wrapped around her like a soft gust.

They were twelve and fifteen, lost in the Carpathians on a hiking trail gone wrong. Their guide had vanished during a sudden rainstorm. Trees towered. The map dissolved in Hannah's soaked hands. But Jacob — wild-haired and soaking wet — had pointed up to the moss, to the bend of the river, to the echo of their voices on the rock.

"We go west," he'd said, calm as a whisper. "The mountain will turn for us if we don't fight it."

They'd made it back, then.

They would make it now.

"Let's go," she said.

They slipped down a side corridor, their shadows long in the dying light.

Behind them, Gara de Nord remained — not just a station, but a palimpsest of all they were walking through: old powers, rewritten borders, and a sibling bond once fractured but quietly reforging.

One empire gone. Another rising.

And between them — blood, trust, and the whispers of a shared past still finding its voice.

—Then we find him first. Or we go down proving he mattered.

Chapter Nine - Chasing Echoes

The private terminal was nestled discreetly at the edge of Otopeni Airport, outside Bucharest, masked from public view by towering, frost-covered pines and concrete walls topped with loops of concertina wire. Hannah and Jacob arrived in silence, the crunch of gravel beneath the car tyres sounding unnaturally loud in the hush of early evening. Beyond the tinted windows lay an expanse of tarmac bathed in dim amber floodlights, empty save for a sleek, nondescript jet that sat patiently, almost expectantly, awaiting their arrival.

Hem's voice whispered discreetly in Jacob's earpiece.

"Surveillance check complete. Frequencies adjusted. Airport systems remain unaware of my monitoring. All clear."

Inside the small terminal, security was swift yet meticulous. Passports exchanged hands with few words spoken, eyes that seemed trained to forget faces the moment they disappeared from view. The building itself exuded an understated luxury—minimalist furnishings, marble surfaces polished to a mirror finish, and artwork abstract enough to reveal nothing.

Minutes later, as they climbed the steps into the private aircraft, Hannah glanced behind her, catching the briefest movement from shadowed figures beyond the glass. Jacob's hand touched her arm lightly, urging her forward.

Settling into plush leather seats facing one another, the hum of the engines started softly, like an orchestral prelude. The plane taxied smoothly before gently ascending, leaving Bucharest's glittering lights fading like stars falling into an ocean of darkness.

"Flight time to Chişinău is approximately one hour," announced the pilot calmly over the intercom.

A quiet attendant approached, offering drinks with a polite, professional smile. Hannah opted for a glass of deep-red Bordeaux, while Jacob chose a single malt whisky, neat, nodding quietly in appreciation as he accepted the tumbler.

Jacob stared out of the window, watching as the ground dissolved beneath a low layer of cloud. The cabin lights dimmed slightly, creating a cocoon of quiet intimacy. Hannah watched her brother, studying the faint lines that traced his temples, evidence of years spent carrying burdens he'd rarely shared.

"Jacob?" Hannah began gently, breaking the long-held silence. She waited until he turned slowly toward her, a question forming in his eyes.

She chose her words carefully, aware of the fragile ground she was treading. "Why didn't you ever come back home? You didn't even come to Mum's funeral."

Jacob looked away, jaw tightening slightly. His fingers drummed softly on the armrest. "It wasn't that simple, Han."

"It never is," she said softly. "But you never gave us—gave me—a chance to understand. Ethan reached out, you know. He tried to mend things. He believed in you, even when you disappeared."

Jacob's throat moved visibly. "I know. Ethan... Ethan always saw through the chaos. He contacted me more than once, especially after the exposé."

"Why didn't you respond? He was trying to help."

Jacob drew a long breath, his voice barely above a whisper. "I couldn't face any of you after what happened. The exposé, the corruption scandal—I thought I was doing the right thing, uncovering the truth. But it spiralled, Hannah. Innocent people got hurt. Good people. Colleagues. Friends. Our family got hurt. Dad lost a business deal he'd spent years cultivating, and Mum... she was so disappointed, it was like I became invisible to her. I thought you'd all be safer, better off, if I stayed away."

The plane gave a gentle lurch, a brief pocket of turbulence that seemed to echo the turbulence within their conversation. Hannah leaned forward, touching his knee briefly, a gesture of reconciliation and quiet strength.

"We all make choices we regret, Jacob. But family... it endures. Ethan always believed in that. He used to say forgiveness is stronger than silence."

Jacob's eyes found hers again, the mask slipping just enough to reveal vulnerability beneath. "Did Ethan ever resent me for not reaching back sooner?"

"No," Hannah said quietly, her gaze steady and sincere. "He admired you, Jacob. He thought you were brave. Flawed, yes, but brave."

Jacob's mouth curled slightly, a ghost of a smile. "Ethan always was generous with second chances. I wish I'd told him that."

"You still might get the chance," Hannah murmured softly, turning her eyes back to the darkness outside, her voice trailing with hope. "He's still guiding us, somehow."

Jacob nodded, silent agreement settling between them, warmer than before. The aircraft descended gently through thinning clouds, Chişinău's sparse lights flickering into view below like distant candles marking uncertain paths. Each pinpoint of light seemed to beckon them forward into deeper mysteries, bringing them closer not only to Ethan's secrets but to truths within themselves long left unspoken.

The plane touched down smoothly, wheels kissing the runway with a quiet sigh of relief. They were closer now, bound by fragile yet strengthening threads, stepping into a city wrapped in echoes waiting to speak.

Chişinău greeted them with a crispness that bit softly at their skin, the air sharp with winter's edge. A waiting car whisked them silently through quiet streets, the ride from the airport to their destination taking roughly twenty minutes.

Hem's discreet voice reassured Jacob,

"Surveillance scans completed. Route clear. Safe house secure."

Outside, glimpses of the city rolled by—a curious blend of stark Soviet-era concrete buildings interspersed with elegant structures influenced by Ottoman and Romanian designs. Street vendors packed away their stalls for the evening, while people gathered inside warmly lit cafés, sipping coffee, laughing, and chatting animatedly. The suburb where their safe house lay was nestled within a historical quarter, its winding streets cobbled and narrow, flanked by softly illuminated lamps casting amber pools of light onto ornate façades with arched windows and intricate balconies.

They arrived at a small, inconspicuous café bustling with locals quietly conversing over pastries and cups of strong, aromatic coffee.

Hem directed Jacob through his earpiece,

"Proceed through the café, rear corridor, second door on the left."

Jacob guided Hannah confidently through the lively café, nodding politely to the barista behind the polished wooden counter who offered a welcoming smile. They went through a narrow, dimly lit staircase that spiralled upward, as directed by Hem. Ethan had hinted subtly about this location in earlier communications, cryptic clues woven into casual conversations about his studies of Ottoman architecture. The flat itself was comfortably minimalist, arranged meticulously—a small living area, two modest bedrooms, and a compact kitchen with vintage tiles.

In the living room, an Ottoman-style carpet covered much of the polished wooden floor. Jacob knelt beside it, tracing the carpet's ornate patterns with his fingers, guided by memory and Ethan's cryptic hint, "truth beneath woven secrets."

After a brief, deliberate inspection, Jacob located a slight irregularity—a hidden latch beneath the edge of the carpet. Pressing it gently, a section of the wooden flooring silently rose, revealing a hidden compartment. Inside, a polished wooden case sealed with red wax, clearly marked with Ethan's initials, awaited discovery. Hannah's pulse quickened as she broke the seal, lifting the lid to reveal an old scroll and sheets of musical notation.

A memory surged vividly, pulling Hannah back to a sunlit afternoon in Istanbul, walking through the museum with Ethan. His fascination with Ottoman music had always amazed her. "Music was never just sound," Ethan had said, eyes alight with discovery. "The Ottomans used it to encode messages, conceal truths. Listen carefully enough, and every note tells you something more."

Jacob's voice pulled her gently from the reverie. "Hem traced the musical cipher. It points to an old conservatory—it's Ana Dumitrescu's research centre now. She's connected deeply with Cedrela."

Hannah nodded, absorbing this revelation. "Ethan trusted her implicitly. If he left these clues, Ana will know how to interpret them."

Jacob examined the case closely, revealing an engraving beneath the lining—an image of a violin intertwined with Ottoman script. His voice carried quiet admiration. "Ethan always said truth lies in harmony."

Their eyes met, both sensing the weight of what they were uncovering, the invisible threads Ethan had meticulously woven around them.

Hem's voice echoed softly through Jacob's earpiece again,

"Coordinates confirmed. Ana Dumitrescu awaits your arrival. Surveillance perimeter secure. No threats detected."

They exchanged a determined glance, knowing their next move was clear. The city's secrets awaited, entwined with their own, deeper and more dangerous than they had imagined.

Stepping out into the chilly Chişinău evening, Hannah and Jacob instinctively drew their coats tighter. Their breath misted softly in the twilight air, carrying a gentle stillness that spoke of forgotten stories. The Historic Centre of Chişinău, known locally as the Ottoman Quarter, was once a bustling heart of trade and diplomacy under Ottoman influence. In its prime, it had been an elegant crossroads where merchants bartered silks and spices, scholars exchanged ideas, and political allegiances were quietly forged. Even now, centuries later, this history lingered like a delicate fragrance, subtly shaping modern Chişinău society through its architecture, cuisine, and collective memory.

Walking through these streets felt like stepping gently through layers of time—past and present entwined delicately. Hannah sensed the whispers of those long gone, the vibrant lives that had thrived beneath the shadow of the Ottoman crescent, their echoes still shaping the city's pulse.

Guided by Hem's discreet instructions, Jacob led Hannah along cobbled lanes to an imposing yet gracefully aged structure—the Zaharia Conservatory, a renowned musical institution dating back to the Ottoman era. Its exterior was an exquisite tapestry of Ottoman motifs: intricately patterned tiles framing arched windows, delicate calligraphy in faded gold script adorning its entrance, and beautifully carved wooden doorways that bore centuries of silent guardianship.

Hannah paused briefly, her eyes tracing the elegant calligraphy. She softly translated aloud for Jacob's benefit, her voice filled with quiet awe: "'Music, a bridge to harmony and truth.' The Ottomans believed music wasn't just entertainment—it was a language, a hidden voice that spoke truths words alone couldn't convey."

Jacob nodded thoughtfully, pushing open the heavy wooden door. Its hinges murmured gently, revealing a softly illuminated interior. Inside, faded yet ornate carpets lined hallways lit warmly by concealed LED lights, carefully preserving the atmosphere of the Ottoman past.

As they stepped into the long corridor, Hannah admired framed sheets of antique music lining the walls, each bearing the signature of composers whose names had long since faded into obscurity. The music itself seemed to breathe softly, holding secrets yet to be revealed.

At the end of the corridor stood Ana Dumitrescu, her figure gracefully poised beneath a delicate Ottoman archway. Her presence felt natural yet commanding. With eyes both sharp and warm, Ana stepped forward, extending a slender hand in greeting.

"Ethan anticipated your arrival," Ana explained gently, noticing Jacob's curious gaze. "He entrusted me with specific instructions and cues. Once Hem detected your access to the Chişinău safe house, your AI established a secure link with me, confirming your presence. Ethan knew you'd rely on Hem—he counted on your methods as much as his own."

Jacob nodded appreciatively, realising Ethan's foresight extended even further than he'd imagined. "Thank you for meeting us."

Ana's gaze shifted warmly to Hannah. "He spoke highly of you. Ethan once told me you were the only person he fully trusted with all his truths."

Hannah felt her heart swell with bittersweet pride. She reached into her bag, carefully presenting the scroll and musical notation. Ana received it reverently, her fingers brushing gently over Ethan's handwritten annotations.

"This is Cedrela," Ana said quietly, eyes tracing the delicate script. "A sophisticated Ottoman musical cipher. It was more than an encryption technique; it represented trust, secrecy, and powerful alliances during Ottoman rule. Music encoded diplomatic messages, trade agreements—even warnings of betrayal."

Ana led them deeper into the conservatory, guiding them into a spacious room filled with advanced technology subtly integrated into its historical setting. She spoke softly, her voice carrying deep respect. "Cedrela was originally an Ottoman political network of influential merchants, diplomats, and scholars operating covertly throughout Moldavia. The network managed trade routes, political stability, and ensured economic prosperity. To ordinary Moldavians, the Ottoman presence meant stability, opportunity, yet also cautious respect born from complex power dynamics."

Jacob watched Ana thoughtfully. "And now? Is Cedrela still active?"

Ana nodded gravely. "Yes, but under different names and disguises. Ethan discovered its modern form—still influential in Moldova's politics and economics, manipulating quietly from the shadows. That knowledge placed him in grave danger."

Her eyes softened with empathy as she handed Hannah a small data drive. "Ethan decoded part of the cipher. But to unlock it completely, he encoded it with something deeply personal. He mentioned only you would understand: 'My mirror in the dark.'"

Hannah drew a sharp breath, memories flooding her mind—a tender night in Istanbul, Ethan's voice murmuring intimately about trust and balance. "It was his secret phrase for me," she admitted quietly. "It meant I reflected truth back to him when everything else seemed uncertain."

Ana nodded solemnly, clearly moved. "Then you're the key, Hannah. Only you can fully decipher Ethan's truths."

Before Hannah could respond further, Jacob flinched slightly, urgently listening as Hem's voice broke through his earpiece.

"Security alert—previous safe house compromised. Immediate departure required."

Jacob exchanged a rapid glance with Hannah, his voice low but decisive. "We need to move, now."

Ana immediately pressed a small device into Jacob's hand. "I anticipated potential risks. There's a car waiting outside, an ally of mine. Use him to get out safely."

Stepping quickly into the night, the city now felt charged with tension. Every shadow, every quiet sound whispered urgency. At the curb, a sleek car idled silently, its tinted windows reflecting the dim streetlights.

Jacob approached cautiously. The driver lowered the window, their eyes meeting in silent confirmation. Jacob relaxed slightly, nodding back at Hannah. "He's Ana's contact. We're safe."

Hannah entered the car swiftly, Jacob following. As the vehicle glided quietly into the darkened streets, she clutched the small drive tightly, heart pounding softly against her chest.

"My mirror in the dark," she whispered softly to herself, determined to unlock Ethan's final secret. She glanced at Jacob, drawing quiet strength from his reassuring presence.

Jacob noticed her thoughtful expression. "We'll figure it out together," he said gently, echoing her thoughts.

"Yes," Hannah replied quietly, her voice resolute despite lingering fears. "Together."

Hannah continued, "Did Ethan always anticipate this? How deep did his preparations go?"

Jacob exhaled slowly, eyes fixed on the shadowy landscape outside. "Ethan understood people. And he trusted our bond—maybe even more than we realised."

She leaned back into her seat, fingers still gripping the small device Ana had provided. "Then let's trust in that bond now, more than ever."

Jacob nodded quietly, the shadows outside blurring softly into darkness, each kilometre taking them further into unknown dangers—and perhaps, closer to the truth Ethan had painstakingly hidden for them to discover.

"Next stop?" the driver asked curtly, eyes meeting Jacob's in the rearview mirror.

"North," Jacob answered firmly, settling in beside Hannah. "Towards Soroca."

The car pulled smoothly into traffic, Chișinău quickly receding behind them, yet the city's echoes followed closely—echoes of Ethan, of secrets, and a betrayal waiting quietly to reveal itself.

—The wasn't decoding the pass, he was preseving it.

Chapter Ten - Threads of History

They left Chișinău just after seven, the conservatory's glow swallowed quickly by the autumn dusk. The driver—a quiet man named Iurie, handpicked by Ana—nodded once at Jacob before pulling into motion. Jacob slid in beside Hannah in the back seat, letting the door click shut behind him. Their driver said nothing, eyes fixed forward, hands resting calmly on the wheel. He looked like someone accustomed to waiting, watching, disappearing. Former intelligence, maybe. Loyal. Jacob didn't need to ask.

Hem's voice entered his earpiece, soft and clear. "Avoid Route E583. Alternative roads selected—low surveillance exposure. Estimated arrival: 10:45 p.m."

Jacob leaned forward slightly, voice low. "Take the north-east bypass through Cricova."

Iurie gave a curt nod and adjusted course without a word.

The city lights faded behind them, replaced by the long hush of the Moldovan countryside. Trees arched over the road like sentinels. Frosted fields stretched into the dark like pages waiting to be written on.

The further they drove, the more Jacob felt the pace of the world shift. Out here, things didn't hum with urgency—they held breath. Villages flickered past in brief vignettes: low-slung cottages painted in soft pastels, blue smoke rising from crooked chimneys. Old women with scarves tied beneath their chins leaned on gates as dogs padded quietly beside them. A donkey cart creaked along a field's edge, silhouetted by the moonlight. It was the kind of stillness that made you feel like you'd wandered behind the world's curtain.

"Next deviation in 2.7 kilometres," Hem said.

Jacob offered soft guidance to Iurie, watching as the driver executed the turns without hesitation. He liked that. Trusted it.

Beside him, Hannah leaned her head against the chilled glass of the window, watching the world dissolve into shadowed hills and narrow bends. There was something elemental about travelling by backroad at night—like threading themselves into history's hidden seams. The air outside was heavy with the kind of cold that demanded respect, the sky above a slate sheet pulled tight with promise and peril.

For a while, neither of them spoke. The road lulled them into quiet introspection, the occasional flick of headlights illuminating hollow barns and shuttered homes nestled against the frostbitten earth.

"You know," Hannah said finally, her voice soft and steady, "Ethan once told me that the original Cedrela routes—the ones the Ottomans used—weren't just about trade. They were about truth. Hidden pathways for information too dangerous for official messengers to carry."

Jacob cast her a glance. "Secret roads for secret truths. Sounds like something he'd chase."

Hannah smiled faintly. "He wasn't chasing, Jacob. He was mapping. Layer by layer. He believed history could be rewritten if the original paths were remembered."

The silence that followed wasn't empty. It was weighted. Jacob kept his eyes on the road, but he felt her words settle in his chest like stones dropped in water. He was starting to see Ethan not just as a man in hiding, but as a man trying to illuminate shadows too wide for one lifetime.

Hem buzzed softly.

"Unknown signal—low-frequency ping—dismissed. Likely agricultural drone telemetry."

Jacob relaxed slightly, tension released from his grip on the edge of the car seat.

They passed through a series of scattered hamlets, each marked by a chipped Orthodox cross or a sagging signpost leaning into the wind. In one village, a single house glowed with a fire's warmth behind lace-curtained windows. In another, an old man walked alone beside the road, leading a cow through the frost as if time hadn't dared ask him to change.

Somewhere just east of Teleneşti, the car's headlights cut through mist rising off the riverbank. The small town they rolled into was quiet, but not asleep—windows flickered with soft lamplight, and the scent of woodsmoke carried on the breeze.

"There," Hannah said, nodding toward a warmly lit sign that read Casa cu Flori. "Let's stop. I need something that isn't adrenaline."

Iurie didn't speak. He slowed the car and pulled up beside the gravelled path with mechanical ease. Jacob was already reaching for the handle.

Casa cu Flori sat like something out of a painting—stone and timber, its roof steep and shingled, with ivy still clinging stubbornly to its outer walls. A wrought-iron gate creaked slightly in the wind. Carved tulips framed the archway above the door, and frost had settled on the windowpanes like lace.

Through the windows, warm lamplight glowed over embroidered curtains. Shadows of people moved within—slow, unhurried. The sound of laughter and a distant violin filtered out when Jacob opened the door for Hannah.

Inside, the warmth was instant and real. The room smelled of firewood, roasted peppers, and garlic butter. The ceiling beams were old and low, hung with dried herbs and embroidered linen. Walls were decorated with framed black-and-white photos—weddings, market days, generations of faces watching from the past. A stone hearth burned brightly, and laughter hummed low beneath it all.

Jacob scanned the room. Locals dotted the tables—three old men playing backgammon, a couple in their twenties eating from a shared plate of mamaliga—its golden softness steaming in the cool air, dotted with tangy white cheese and a curl of roasted pepper. The scent of warm cornmeal and sour cream lingered in the breeze, a quiet comfort in a street still holding its breath. It wasn't tourist-warm. It was home-warm and it was the kind of place where strangers passed without fuss, provided they asked no questions.

Hannah and Jacob settled into a table near the fire, warmth curling up their legs, while Iurie found a seat on the bar in a corner.

The hostess, a cheerful woman in a thick wool apron, approached their table with a gentle smile. "Zeamă and bread. Wine?"

Jacob answered, "Please."

The soup arrived hot and fragrant—lemony chicken broth laced with parsley and dill. Garlic rubbed over crisp rye. Red wine deep and warm.

For a time, they ate in quiet. Jacob watched the fire dance across Hannah's face, softening the lines drawn by grief and fatigue. They were simply siblings at dinner. No ghosts. No codes. Just the silence between them softening into something resembling peace.

She looked up suddenly. "You alright?"

He gave a soft nod. "Thinking. About Ethan. About how familiar this feels."

She smiled faintly. "Ethan would've loved this place. Probably already catalogued the spice ratios in his notes."

Jacob chuckled under his breath. "He said broth reflected belief. Each village had its own truths. You could taste them."

"This place," Hannah continued, looking around, "feels like the kind of inn Ottoman emissaries would have stopped in. A neutral zone, somewhere between kingdoms and intentions."

From the far end of the room, an elderly man observed them. Not rudely—just a quiet, knowing gaze. Jacob met it for a moment, then let it pass.

Hem whispered again.

"Road ahead clear. No known signal interference. ETA to Soroca adjusted: 11:15 p.m."

Jacob left cash neatly folded beneath his glass. Iurie was already standing outside near the car, unmoving but alert.

They stepped back into the cold. The fog had thickened, wrapping the village in soft gauze. Headlights cut through like twin blades. Jacob opened the back door for Hannah. She stepped in silently, pulling her coat closer.

Jacob followed, settling beside her as Iurie climbed back in without a word.

"Soroca," Jacob said quietly.

The car moved forward, its hum steady and low, as the village faded behind them. The road stretched on—black, winding, and waiting.

Ahead, the fortress stood in silence, cloaked in shadow.

And history was about to speak.

They left Casa cu Flori just after nine, the road curling north through hills that breathed mist and memory. The car rolled on steadily, tyres humming against uneven tarmac, the headlights slicing through shadowed groves and frost-lined hedges. Jacob sat silent, letting Hem's navigation hum in the background while Iurie focused on the road ahead, ever composed, ever alert.

Hannah leaned toward the window again, her voice low but animated. "We're passing through part of the old Cantacuzino trail," she said. "That castle, just west of this route—Cantacuzino Castle—was built by one of the oldest noble families in the region. Ottoman allies, technically, but also intermediaries. They built it as both a retreat and a message."

Jacob glanced at her reflection. "What kind of message?"

"That culture could outlast conquest," she replied, her finger drawing shapes in the condensation on the glass. "Even under the Sultan's influence, they preserved Romanian language, local craftsmanship. Cantacuzino Castle wasn't just a home—it was a quiet rebellion, dressed in elegance."

The road rose into higher ground, and for a brief moment the fog parted, revealing the Caraiman Crossing below—a vast sweep of land where the forests dipped and the road split like an artery, bordered by low walls of carved stone and tangled hedgerows. A soft breeze stirred the treetops, and in the distance, a single stork's silhouette perched atop a wooden pole.

"Caraiman was once a critical crossing," Hannah continued. "Caravans moving north toward Polish territory. But during the Ottoman period, it became a monitoring point. Tolls were collected here. Intelligence passed quietly. Some say decisions made at Caraiman redrew maps more than once."

Jacob raised a brow. "And we're just... gliding through it."

"We're never just passing through history," she murmured. "We're always inside it."

The road sloped down again, winding toward the river, and by the time they approached Soroca, the town shimmered beneath a thin gauze of mist. The Dniester flowed quietly in the dark, its surface catching fragments of moonlight like silvered ink. Once a Cold War boundary and silent witness to vanished regimes, its waters had ferried everything from exiles to secrets—now it carried only the weight of memory. And there, rising solemnly at the edge—Soroca Fortress, timeless and still, its round towers rising like echo chambers for the past.

Hannah whispered, "It looks like something out of a myth."

Jacob nodded. "That's exactly what Ethan called it. 'The Ottoman palimpsest.' Said every empire that touched it left something behind."

Iurie turned down a quiet cobbled street, gliding into the heart of the old quarter. Soroca slept beneath its veil—shutters drawn, lanterns dim, a town folded neatly into itself. But beneath the stillness, something pulsed. A kind of waiting.

Hem buzzed.

"Surveillance sweep complete. No heat anomalies. One active data ping—local node near central fortress square. Unregistered."

"Could be our contact," Jacob said. "Could be something else."

The inn stood just off the square—a two-storey limestone structure whose elegance came not from grandeur, but endurance. Hanul de Piatră had stood for nearly four centuries. It had once been a waystation for Ottoman envoys, and during the Treaty of Vaslui negotiations in 1473, it served briefly as neutral diplomatic refuge after Prince Stephen's resistance pushed into this region.

Jacob recalled Ethan mentioning that fact—how the carved tulips over the door matched those found in Ottoman guesthouses as far south as Anatolia.

They stepped out of the car, fog curling at their ankles. The air held the scent of river stone, old wood, and the faint bite of coming rain. Iurie opened the boot and passed them their bags without a word.

The innkeeper, a greying man in wool slippers, greeted them without question. "Room upstairs. Second door on the right. Coffee before dawn if you want it." And the innkeeper escorted Iurie to the back quarters to his room for the night. Iurie nodded to Jacob before they went on their ways.

Inside, the hall curved gently, its plaster walls bowed with age. The runner muffled their steps as they climbed. Hannah's fingers brushed the carved railing, her eyes scanning etched medallions of olive branches, musical instruments, and interlocking crescents.

"These were Ottoman diplomatic symbols," she murmured. "Carved by stonemasons who not only spoke three languages but only swore allegiance to stone.These were carved during the Phanariot period, Ottoman governors stationed here—this was one of their safehouses. The design matches what Ethan noted in his fieldwork."

84

Their room was simple: two single beds, a small writing desk, and heavy curtains drawn against the night. The radiator hissed softly, the kind of sound that made space feel lived in. A ceramic stove stood in one corner, unused but dignified.

Jacob dropped their bags quietly. "We rest a few hours, then find Dragu."

Hannah didn't answer right away. She moved toward the window, drawing the curtain just slightly. The fortress loomed in the distance, half-consumed by mist. Beyond it, the fortress stood still, shrouded in mist, looming like a secret waiting to be spoken.

"Ethan stood here," she said. "I can feel it."

Jacob looked at her reflection in the window. She wasn't grieving. She was certain.

Hem chimed again, this time softer.

> "Dragu confirmed. Meeting at 08:00. Location: fortress
> wall, west archway. Signal traced to university network."

"Right on time," Jacob muttered.

He glanced at Hannah. "We sleep in shifts?"

"You first," he said. "I'll wake you if the ghosts get chatty."

She smiled faintly and crawled beneath the quilt, already turning inward.

As he sat near the desk, Jacob let his eyes drift to the old map framed on the far wall—Moldavia drawn in Ottoman script, trade routes stitched like veins across a long-forgotten body. One of the lines terminated here, in Soroca.

He followed it with his finger, tracing the path Ethan might've taken.

Somewhere, along that ancient road, the truth waited.

And in the morning, they'd walk straight toward it.

The morning in Soroca was mist-stitched and quiet, as though the town had pulled a woollen shawl over its shoulders and gone back to sleep. The air was damp but gentle, kissed with woodsmoke and the scent of wet limestone. Golden leaves scattered across the cobbled street like forgotten letters.

Jacob stood at the window of their inn room, towel looped around his neck, hair damp from the shower. He sipped slowly from the ceramic cup in his hand, letting the steam and bitter coffee stir him fully awake. Below, the fortress loomed in silhouette—its round towers still half-shrouded by fog, like the ghosts of soldiers refusing to retreat.

Behind him, Hannah pulled on her coat, already alert after her night watch. She handed him another cup.

"Drink up," she said softly. "Professor Dragu doesn't strike me as someone who waits."

Jacob smirked. "That makes two of you."

The walk to the fortress took them past shuttered shopfronts and flower boxes lined with drying marigolds. The west archway, their meeting point, was a towering structure of weathered stone and sunken carvings, its iron studs slick with morning dew. Moss lined the lower stones, and ivy crept along the edges like ancient veins. A small metal lantern swung gently beside the gate, its flame fighting the fog.

Hannah slowed, letting her fingertips brush against a crest embedded in the wall—crescent moon, olive branch, a single tulip petal. She recognised the symbolism instantly.

"Cedrela," she whispered. "Ottoman courier seal. They marked safehouses this way."

Jacob stepped closer. "How do you still remember all this?"

"Because Ethan said truth leaves a pattern. You just have to look long enough."

The gate creaked open, and there he was—Professor Ilie Dragu, framed like a memory beneath the arch.

He wore a dark coat and a Ben Hogan cap pulled neatly over his silver hair. A leather satchel hung at his side. His face was lined but warm, with eyes that had once devoured knowledge but now simply understood it.

"Hannah Goldstein," he said, extending a gloved hand. "And Jacob Adler. It's strange meeting the voices behind Ethan's most guarded correspondence."

Hannah's breath caught. Unmistakeable. That was the word he hadn't said, but she heard it anyway. Her pulse shifted—something between pride and fear.

"Ethan described us?" she asked.

Dragu smiled faintly. "Not in words exactly. But his silence was specific. The way one might leave a name out only because it mattered too much to risk."

Jacob tilted his head. "Charming. And vague."

Dragu gestured them forward. "Come. There's a chamber beneath the tower. I've kept it undisturbed."

The stone staircase spiralled downward, each step worn smooth by centuries of passage. The air grew colder. Walls lined with faded murals curved inward. One showed a scribe hunched over sheet music, surrounded by flames, yet untouched. Another bore the marks of deliberate chisel work—someone had tried to erase it.

They entered a small archive room lined with shelves and a single reading desk near a slit-window overlooking the river. The space smelled of dust and metal and the faintest trace of cedar.

Dragu moved to an old wooden cabinet, rummaging through a drawer before pulling out a folded receipt. He held it up.

"Here," he said. "The courier company—Danube Transit. I never caught the courier's name. Ethan was... secretive, even in the way he trusted me."

He retrieved a linen-wrapped folder from the cabinet and placed it on the desk.

"I was told never to open it. Only to wait."

Hannah unwrapped the folder slowly. Inside: annotated sheet music, diagrams of domes, mathematical notations, and a separate folded letter in Ethan's handwriting. She opened it with steady fingers.

"Cedrela does not hide. It harmonises in silence."

As she read, a whisper of Ethan's voice echoed in her memory—a recording she'd once overheard in a university lab, stored in a backup file marked "Fragment.ETH-7."

> "Harmony exists where chaos can't breathe. If you're decoding this, you've already chosen to remember what the world forgot."

Hem pinged softly in Jacob's ear. Jacob blinked, then adjusted his smart glasses—sleek, ordinary-looking, but fitted with discreet AR overlays. Through them, Hem could scan visible metadata embedded in each document.

> "Alert: Metadata anomaly. Timestamp—four months before Ethan's disappearance. Passive shortwave tag identified."

Jacob frowned. "This page," he said, lifting one of the diagrams. "It's broadcasting."

"Broadcasting what?" Hannah asked.

"Not content—location."

Hem whispered again:

> "Transmission handshake detected. Minimal packet. Location broadcast sent. Shortwave, encrypted."

Jacob snapped open his multitool, flipped the diagram, and scraped gently beneath a fold—revealing a small micro-emitter no larger than a fingernail.

"Tracker," he muttered. "And not from Ethan."

Dragu looked stunned. "That wasn't there when I received it. I swear it."

"Who delivered it?" Jacob asked, calmly but firmly.

Dragu reached for the receipt again. "Danube Transit. No name. No voice. He wore gloves. Sunglasses. Just said it was from Istanbul."

Hannah folded Ethan's note, her expression unreadable. "Ethan didn't send this to be safe. He sent it to be followed."

Hem's voice again:

"Intercept sequence aborted. Location partially masked. But not in time."

Jacob turned to Hannah. "Someone else was meant to intercept this."

She closed the folder slowly, then looked up at the fortress walls.

"Then we've just stepped into someone else's conversation."

—She closed the door. The echoes followed.

Chapter Eleven - The Turning Point

The radiator in their inn room clicked faintly as the heat cycled on, casting small pops into the early light. Jacob sat at the edge of the bed, lacing his boots slowly. The coffee on the nightstand had long since cooled. Morning mist still clung to the windows, but sunlight was starting to push through.

Across the room, Hannah sat at the desk, laptop open, headphones on. She paused the audio, adjusted a setting, then leaned in again. Her eyes were sharp, scanning not just for sound—but for meaning.

"It's not just a message," she said at last. "There's something woven underneath Ethan's voice."

Jacob stood and moved beside her. She hit play again.

Ethan's voice returned—measured and calm:

> "Harmony exists where chaos can't breathe. If you're decoding this, you've already chosen to remember what the world forgot."

Then came it: a faint background pattern—not speech, not static. Music. A melody stitched behind the words like embroidery behind canvas.

"Not random," Hannah said. "That's an eastern scale—an Ottoman lament."

Jacob frowned. "Leyla?"

She nodded slowly. "It's the one she used in her final lecture series. Ethan quoted it once in a paper draft he never published."

Jacob leaned over slightly. "He built it for her."

Hem pinged softly in Jacob's ear.

"Pattern complexity exceeds passive analysis. Unusual tonal structure. Recommend activation of sandbox AI for deeper decryption."

Jacob blinked. "You're suggesting Nex?"

"Affirmative. Parameters align with Nex's core structure."

Jacob hesitated—then nodded. "Do it."

A moment passed. Then a new voice entered—quieter, smoother, with a shadowed edge.

"Decryption accepted. Musical identity signature recognised. Generating layered structure. Message integrity: 87%."

Nex had returned. Not because Ethan planted him—but because Ethan's cipher was too personal, too intricate, too emotionally encoded for anything less.

Jacob straightened. "He didn't mean to leave us a puzzle. He left a map."

Downstairs, Iurie had been waiting by the front window since dawn—coat on, bag beside his feet, eyes scanning the quiet courtyard. He hadn't asked for instruction, only assumed there would be one.

Jacob found him sipping slowly from a small glass of tea, as though the world moved at a different speed when he chose it to.

"We'll need to leave shortly," Jacob said.

Iurie nodded once. "Destination?"

"Chişinău. Quiet route. Same discretion."

"You'll have it."

Jacob lingered a moment. "Thanks for waiting."

"I was told your journey wouldn't be short."

Back upstairs, Hannah zipped the folder shut and tucked it into her shoulder bag. She paused at the window.

"It looks different now," she said.

Jacob joined her. Outside, Soroca had awakened. Sunlight bathed the town in warm tones. Market stalls were being set up in the square. Bread carts rolled over the cobbles. Children raced each other past shuttered courtyards, their shouts bouncing off limestone walls.

Hanul de Piatră no longer whispered with mystery—it stood solid in the light, its walls bright and worn like parchment left open on a table. What had been shadowed the night before was now drawn in full relief. The carved tulips, the arched lintels, the mosaic patchwork of centuries etched into stone—it had always been a place of memory. Now it was a place to leave one behind.

Jacob took one last glance as he picked up the folder.

"And now it's behind us."

They stepped out, the door clicking shut behind them, as Nex waited quietly in the lines of the next track, and the road ahead bent just enough to hide what came next.

Nex pinged first in Jacob's ear.

"Auditory trigger confirmed. Signature consistent with prior fragment. Sequence awaiting continuation."

Then Hem followed.

"Route recalculated. Destination secure. Travel time to Chişinău: two hours, thirty-one minutes. Surveillance exposure: minimal along main highway."

They left Soroca just before eleven, the fortress growing smaller in the rearview mirror until it was no more than stone and shadow pressed into the horizon. Jacob sat silent in the backseat, watching the landscape blur. Hannah sat beside him, folder in her lap, headphones still half on, listening to silence between Ethan's notes.

The road to Chişinău curled smooth through the low hills along the R14 and R6 highways. The countryside unrolled like a quiet hymn—fields of tilled soil, rows of birch flickering gold, and the skeletal remains of sunflower stalks bowed in farewell to summer. They passed roadside stalls selling garlic in tight braids, smoked plums in jars, and cheese bundled in waxed linen. Every few kilometres, small villages drifted past like old stories—whitewashed cottages, carved wooden fences, the scent of firewood curling up from chimneys.

As they approached the city limits, Hem pinged again.

"Meeting location confirmed. Muzeul Ținutului. Entry approved. Meeting time: 13:45."

Iurie dropped them near the Muzeul Ținutului, the Museum of the Land—a nineteenth-century mansion-turned-research centre nestled between oak-lined boulevards and rusting electric tram lines. Once a regional seat of Ottoman administration, it now held rotating exhibitions on folk music, political uprisings, and buried artefacts.

The museum's heavy doors bore an iron filigree, and beneath the lintel, faded Ottoman inscriptions were still visible—words half-scraped by time and revolutions. The air inside was cool and faintly perfumed with old stone, beeswax, and forgotten paper.

Hem scanned the interior before they stepped in.

> "Structure clear. No detectable threats. Vicinity includes four museum staff, two maintenance personnel, no surveillance anomalies."

They entered the east wing. An archivist nodded silently and gestured them through to a private research room—walled in timber, its tall windows filtering in quiet light.

Leyla stood at the far end of the room beside a long table scattered with documents and tuning forks. She was dressed in soft greys and navy, with a scarf wrapped around her neck like a thought she hadn't quite finished thinking. Her dark hair had silver at the edges now, and her hands moved with the calm grace of someone used to holding fragile things.

She turned as they entered, her expression unreadable.

"Hannah," she said.

Hannah's breath caught in her chest. A memory surfaced unbidden.

FLASHBACK

Istanbul, years ago. A narrow rooftop terrace.

Ethan, holding two glasses of çay, barefoot, hair damp from the shower. Leyla sat with a book open on her lap, Hannah cross-legged on a rug across from them.

"Leyla's the one who shows me the notes," Ethan had said, handing Hannah her cup. "But you—" he tapped the side of his head gently, "—you're the only one who hears the whole song."

Back in the room, Hannah blinked once. The air felt thinner.

"Hello, Leyla," she said. The words didn't sound like hers.

For a moment, the two women stood still—something between recognition and reckoning passing between them.

Leyla's expression was hard to read—part caution, part something else. Her eyes shimmered, just briefly, then steadied.

"You look like him when you're tired," she said. "But you speak like your father."

Jacob moved to the table. "Let's get to it."

Leyla smiled, just enough. "And you must be Jacob. I've heard only the most evasive mentions of you."

"I tend to prefer it that way."

Leyla nodded. Both Hannah and Leyla moved to the table joining Jacob. Spread before them were three pages of dense musical notation, overlaid with handwritten annotations in Ottoman script. Leyla unrolled a sheet of annotated musical notation. A second document followed—a photograph was tucked into one corner—Ethan standing beside a cracked mural in an old lecture hall, smiling like he knew something he'd never tell.

"I held this for years," she said. "He never told me exactly what it meant. Only that if this ever made it into your hands, it would mean he'd stopped speaking out loud."

Jacob picked up the sheet. Nex pinged immediately.

"Signature recognised. Cross-match confirmed. Notation includes mirrored cipher. Emotional pattern present."

Leyla glanced at her. "He encoded feelings. That was his evolution. He stopped recording facts and started recording grief."

Hem added:

"Ink on second sheet inconsistent. Origin: Istanbul, Project Lale archives. Courier unidentified."

Jacob tensed. "When did you receive that page?"

Leyla hesitated. "A week before Ethan disappeared. No note. Just this envelope."

Jacob turned the page. A second melody line had been written in—fainter, faster, as though the composer didn't have time to correct it.

Nex's voice followed, softer.

"Melodic alignment detected. Partial cipher match to prior sequence. Embedded pattern may trigger deeper structure." "Sequence is incomplete. It's waiting for a key."

Leyla stepped back. "That key may be you, Hannah. Or something he left only you would understand."

Hannah lowered the page, her hands trembling slightly now. "Then we find the rest of the melody."

Hannah picked up the sheet. "This melody—he referenced it in one of the recordings. Nex just matched it."

Leyla watched her closely. "It's what we used to call a pivot key. In Cedrela, a melody could do more than convey meaning—it could shift interpretation entirely. Ethan believed sound held memory differently than ink."

Jacob asked, "Why leave this with you?"

Leyla looked at him now. "Because he knew you wouldn't trust me."

Jacob's eyes narrowed slightly.

"I don't blame you," she added. "But I'm not here to rewrite Ethan's story. I'm just here because he asked me to hold a piece of it."

Hannah gently turned over the last page. Tucked beneath it, nearly folded into the crease, was a short musical phrase scrawled hastily in a different hand. Less precise. Urgent.

She held it up. "This wasn't his."

Leyla stepped closer. "No. That wasn't in the original packet. It came later. No signature. No return address."

Jacob exchanged a look with Hannah.

Hem's voice again:

"Ink composition scanned. Origin: Istanbul. Archival batch identified as Project Lale acquisition, 2016. Courier unknown."

Nex added quietly:

"This signature was meant to be found. But not yet decoded. The rhythm is... anticipatory."

Hannah folded the page carefully. "Then we're reading it too early."

Leyla stepped back. "Or exactly when someone wants you to."

Outside, the light shifted. A breeze stirred the museum's curtains. Something unspoken pressed into the room like music just beyond hearing. The piano in the corner, untouched for years, seemed to vibrate faintly. A tone left hanging. Waiting.

And the conversation Ethan had started long ago began to hum again between them.

Hannah moved to the upright piano in the corner. Its lid was coated in a fine film of dust. She lifted it slowly, her fingers hovering just above the keys.

"I don't know the full melody," she murmured. "But I remember the phrasing. Ethan always said the pattern wasn't linear—it moved like memory."

Leyla approached quietly. "He believed you'd play it before you understood it."

Jacob glanced toward the door, unsettled. Hem hadn't pinged in a while, and Nex had gone quiet—too quiet.

Hannah pressed the first note. Then another. And another.

The sound rang out, soft but clear. Not quite in tune. But something beneath the surface of the music shifted the room. The window curtains stirred even though the air had stilled. Jacob's ears caught a tone beneath the tone—something that didn't come from the piano.

Nex's voice returned.

> "Secondary sequence detected. Activating emotional decryption stream. Memory capsule linked to Cedrela anchor tone."

Then Ethan's voice filled the room—not from a speaker, not from the laptop. From the walls.

> "If you're hearing this, I've failed to deliver it myself. And that means someone's listening who shouldn't be."

Hannah's hands froze on the keys.

"Cedrela was never just code. It was trust. Memory with teeth. If they have this, then t they're closer than you know."

Jacob moved to the door, eyes scanning the corridor. Hem pinged.

"Audio source embedded in wall conduit. Signal flare detected—echo transmission active. Outbound ping. Directional trace."

Leyla backed away slowly. "Someone tagged the playback. It's transmitting."

Jacob spun. "Can you stop it?"

"Only by finishing it," Hannah said, breathless. "He coded the silence as much as the sound."

She pressed forward, playing the next progression.

The melody shifted—richer now, full of minor chords and restraint, like someone trying not to break.

Ethan's voice returned.

"There's a list. You'll find it where the bells used to ring. Where harmony was outlawed. Where silence was enforced by decree."

Hem pinged again.

"Encrypted relay triggered. Transmitter location—roofline antenna. Signal intercepted en route. Source unknown."

Jacob cursed under his breath. "Someone just tried to trace us."

He reached for the wall, found the seam where the transmitter had been tucked, and yanked it out—an innocuous silver thread no thicker than a vine. He crushed it in his hand.

Nex whispered.

"Data transfer incomplete. But signal handshake acknowledged. Someone knows you were here."

The room was still again. The air seemed to hold its breath.

Leyla's voice was a whisper. "During the Ottoman occupation of Iași, the bell tower was silenced. Music forbidden. Cedrela first emerged there—passed between scribes, lute makers, and women who encoded it into their weaving. It survived not by force, but by... resonance."

Hannah rose slowly, her hand trembling slightly on the piano lid.

Jacob stepped toward her. "You okay?"

She nodded, but her voice was low. "He left me grief wrapped in melody. And a direction inside a wound."

Leyla placed a hand over the sheet music. "You were always the note he never wanted to resolve."

Hannah closed the lid gently. "Then it's time to follow the silence."

They gathered the sheets, folding them into Hannah's bag with deliberate care. The melody Ethan had left behind still echoed faintly in the floorboards, in the arches of the room, in the quiet space between memory and momentum.

Outside, the wind picked up, pushing hard against the windows.

Jacob opened the door.

"Next stop?" he asked.

Hannah didn't look back. "Where the bells were silenced."

"He trusted us to find it," Hannah said quietly. "Even when he didn't trust the world."

And behind them, the room sighed shut—one voice dimming, another rising.

—It had begun.

Chapter Twelve - The Archive Below

It had been four days since Jacob arrived at Hannah's apartment in Bebek—four days since that final, unfinished message from Ethan shattered what little peace she'd rebuilt. In that time, they had crossed three borders, travelled by train, car, and instinct, and uncovered more questions than answers. The deeper they went, the more Cedrela stopped feeling like a cipher—and started to feel like a legacy.

They'd boarded the train mid-afternoon from Chişinău Central Station, a building steeped in Ottoman lineage—built as a critical node in the trade network that once linked Bessarabia to the Rumelia Eyalet. Moorish arches framed soot-darkened mosaics above faded stained-glass windows. In Ottoman times, it was a hub for silks and signatures—today, it served as a bridge between generations: students, vendors, priests, smugglers, and historians crossing each other without knowing.

Before boarding, they made a short detour near the market square. Travelling light had caught up with them, and the clothing shop tucked between an old apothecary and a bookstand off Strada Ismail provided them both with clean trousers, warm shirts, and heavier jackets. Hannah chose a charcoal-grey coat, Jacob a worn leather one with deep pockets. Practical. Forgettable.

Chisinau's terminal itself was grand in a worn, dignified way. Its pillared façade was chipped, its mosaics dulled by soot, but the arched iron windows still caught the sun like stained glass. Inside, a brass plaque commemorated the Ottoman-Russian crossings of the 1800s. Beneath it, a group of musicians played low, lilting violin pieces that made the space feel suspended in time.

Leyla had walked them to the platform but did not join them.

"I'm heading to Bucharest," she'd said, eyes darting to the board. "There's someone I need to speak with—someone Ethan once trusted, but not openly."

Hannah nodded. "Will you stay in contact?"

"If I can."

They exchanged a brief look—not closure, not friendship, just a mutual pause in the middle of unfinished truths.

They arrived in Iași just before dusk, the train's metal frame hissing against the rails like a reluctant breath. The station was older than Chișinău's but bore the same echoes of history—walls once scrawled in Ottoman script, now bearing plaques in Romanian, Moldovan, and Romani. Outside, the city unfolded in a mixture of Orthodox domes and Ottoman remnants, its hills softened by mist and memory.

Now, the platform beneath their boots felt older than the city itself. Iași was a city built on echo. Layers of empire, resistance, poetry, and prayer. Orthodox bells once rang beside Ottoman minarets—until the Phanariot period, when the governors from Constantinople arrived and the bell towers were silenced by decree. Sound was control. Silence, strategy.

Hem pinged softly in Jacob's ear.

"Surveillance level: moderate. Local traffic network linked to two state-run archives. One recent signal matched Cedrela variation. Timestamp: 36 hours ago."

Jacob scanned the station slowly. "We're not the first."

Nex added, his tone almost reverent.

"City housed second Cedrela node. Golia bell tower. Silenced under decree, 1731. Ottoman registry: Yash. Rumelia Eyalet, Upper Moldavia."

"Iași," Hannah said quietly. "We were here once. Ethan said the word to me here. Cedrela."

Jacob looked at her. "Here? Why?"

FLASHBACK

It wasn't in Iași the first time Ethan spoke of Cedrela. It was on a night years ago, during a post-dinner walk along the Bosphorus. The city glowed on both sides of the strait, gold and silver stitched into the water. Ethan had stopped beside a crumbling wall beneath the Çırağan Palace and pointed to an engraving—barely visible.

"That's a tulip," he'd said.

Hannah had squinted at it. "A flower?"

"Not just a flower. A code. They used to mark messages in it. Music, too. Cedrela." He said the word like it was a secret in his mouth.

"What is it?"

"A way to remember without writing anything down."

She hadn't thought about that moment in years—not until now.

They checked into a modest inn near the Trei Ierarhi Church, a place steeped in whispered history and cinnamon tea. The innkeeper, a kind-eyed woman with a scarf wrapped tightly around her silver bun, asked no questions when Jacob requested a room with high walls and low visibility.

As they climbed the narrow stairs, Hannah said, "Ethan said the name like it was made of silk. Like he was afraid it might fall apart if he said it twice."

Jacob replied, "And now it's leading us into bell towers and surveillance fields."

They entered the room—a sparse but warm space with clay walls, an oil lamp on the desk, and a window that opened onto a courtyard shaded by linden trees.

Hem pinged again.

"Historical location identified: Golia Monastery. Bell tower access permitted until 8 PM. Area unmonitored. Probability of target artefact below threshold: 68%."

"Close enough," Jacob muttered. He turned to Hannah. "We go now."

The walk to the Golia Monastery took fifteen minutes. The streets were narrower here. Iași's old quarter held its breath. Stone arches wept moss. Statues of saints, chipped and tired, kept vigil above doorways. A child sat on the curb humming a song his grandmother likely hummed before the Soviets came. As they moved through Iași's older quarter, the mood of the city changed. Tourists gave way to poets, street musicians, and elderly women laying coins at the feet of saints etched in stone. The bell tower rose before them like a watchtower from another lifetime—elegant, weather-stained, and silent. It had rung for centuries until it was ordered quiet. Beneath its stones, resistance didn't shout. It hummed.

Hannah paused at the gate. Her fingers brushed the wall—rough limestone scored with centuries of wear.

"They silenced it here," she said quietly. "During the Phanariot period, when the Ottoman governors ruled. The bells were outlawed. Sound meant gathering. Resistance. Cedrela didn't begin as rebellion—it began as preservation."

Jacob said nothing, only looked up at the tower. A tulip symbol, carved in faded relief, curled around the edge of the base stone. Familiar. Intentional.

Inside, the monastery grounds were hushed. Crows moved between the arches, and the shadows grew deeper as the sun bowed behind the trees.

Hem pinged once more.

"Entry clear. No present surveillance. Acoustics consistent with prior Cedrela signal sites."

Jacob glanced at Hannah. "Let's go below."

They stepped into the place where history wasn't stored—it waited.

Where bells once silenced now echoed in the bones of the floor.

Where Ethan's melody was buried deeper than memory.

The Golia Monastery stood like a sentinel at the edge of Iași's old quarter—its thick walls weathered by centuries of quiet resilience. The courtyard opened wide beneath a cold dusk sky, framed by stone archways and ivy-covered façades. A few visitors lingered near the bell tower, murmuring in low tones, as if the monastery's history demanded reverence even from the unfaithful.

The bell tower itself rose like a final verse—forty-five metres tall, watchful, dignified. Its square Moldavian base flared upward into a soft dome, crowned with an Orthodox cross. Yet, beneath the Christian geometry, traces of Ottoman subtlety clung—curved decorative insets, hand-carved tulip motifs, arching frames along the cloister, all whispering of a time when the building stood not just for faith, but for survival.

Built in the 17th century and fortified during the Phanariot period, the monastery had witnessed centuries of transition: from sanctuary to surveillance, from faith to function. In Ottoman times, the bells were silenced under edict—gatherings discouraged, songs forgotten, and resistance encoded not in revolt, but in silence. Monks turned to copying lost scores in ciphered ink, and sound became a language only the devoted could decode.

Today, the monastery still functioned as a working religious community—a handful of monks maintained services, while tourists moved respectfully through its grounds, drawn by the height of the tower and the weight of its past.

As Hannah and Jacob stepped through the gate, the wind shifted—carrying incense and the scent of old wood and snow-damp stone. Tourists had thinned with the dusk. They had a window to get in before the bells were tolled one last time before closing. The crows had returned to the bell tower's ledges.

Jacob looked up. "It's watching us."

Hannah nodded. "It remembers."

Jacob eyed the path to the bell tower. "Lights are still on."

"Not for long," Hannah said. "They close up soon."

The guard's station was empty. Past the roped-off corridor behind the tower, they found an old iron gate tucked near a crumbling tool shed. Locked, but not complicated.

Jacob bent down, picked it in seconds. No alarms. No motion sensors.

As they stepped beyond the threshold, official lighting gave way to shadow. This part of the monastery wasn't public. It wasn't forbidden—but it had been forgotten. The staircase spiralled downward, narrow and uneven, smoothed by time and footsteps erased from record. The walls were thick with dust and etched faintly with patterns—some deliberate, some accidental.

Hem activated Jacob's smartglasses.

"Interior mapping initiated. Depth estimated: three levels. Temperature variance minimal. No current electromagnetic interference."

Jacob went first. Hannah followed, her hand brushing the wall for balance, fingertips gliding over faint ridges—scratches, carvings, worn glyphs that didn't speak, but remembered.

Nex chimed in, soft but clear.

"Detected pattern match: tulip motif. Ottoman-period shorthand. Symbol group associated with coded musical doctrine—Cedrela, class 2."

The air grew denser the farther they descended. It didn't smell of death. It smelled of restraint—like something had been held here. A truth, folded and hidden, rather than buried.

At the base of the stairs, they reached a low vaulted chamber with walls of carved brick and arched alcoves. Dust shimmered in the light from Jacob's torch. The room was silent—but it felt tuned, as though it was waiting for sound to enter and settle into place.

Against the far wall stood a small desk, half-rotted, draped in a cracked oilskin sheet. Underneath, instruments lay curled in faded linen: an oud, a wooden flute, and several pages of tightly folded parchment. Above the desk, a faint tulip had been etched into the plaster—nearly erased by time, but not quite.

Hannah stepped toward it. "This wasn't a storeroom."

Jacob nodded slowly. "It was a practice room."

Hem scanned the alcoves.

"Residual audio imprint detected. Three unique tonal echoes. Frequencies consistent with early Ottoman scales—Makam Hüzzam and Rast."

Nex followed, a shade slower.

"These aren't just notes. They're relational phrases. Codified intention. Cedrela in emotional context—grief, concealment, warning."

Hannah frowned, frustration rising." He said 'To be opened only when silence breaks' - but there is nothing here."

Jacob straightened. "Hem - scan the room."

Hem's voice responded almost instantly.

"Material density inconsistent. Composite echo behind northern quadrant. Hidden recess—three centimetres behind plaster etching."

Jacob moved toward the tulip. Its lines were faded, but deliberate.

Jacob reached out, tapped the edge. The plaster gave slightly. A recessed niche clicked open with a quiet scrape of stone on stone.

Inside: a wax-sealed envelope, its seal intact, bearing Ethan's initials.

Hannah reached for the envelope, hands steady but cold.

"To be opened only when silence breaks." she said it again.

She broke the seal. A single page of manuscript, and a phrase in Ethan's hand:

"If you're reading this, it means the conversation has turned. Cedrela was never just a cipher. It was a memory structure. A pattern too dangerous for words. The melody leads, but only the silence reveals."

Jacob examined the cloth bundle. Inside was a sheet of unlined paper—blank, except for four small ink dots arranged in a curve. Beneath it, faint etchings on the parchment: numbers, layered against glyphs neither of them recognised.

Nex hummed gently.

"Sequence matches format of encoded auditory locks. This is a trigger sheet. Likely tied to embedded Cedrela fragment. One-time activation."

Hem added:

"Auditory key likely required to initiate full sequence. Suggest locating sound instrument used in original encoding."

Jacob turned to the instruments. "One of these?"

Nex confirmed.

"Flute or oud. Prefer oud."

Hannah knelt beside the oud. Its strings were broken. She touched the frame gently, then closed her eyes and traced her fingers along its edge.

She remembered the sound—not from this place, but from Ethan's apartment in Istanbul. The same melody, hummed late at night, when he thought she wasn't listening.

"Cedrela is personal," she whispered. "That's why it always felt like a person. It held his silence."

Jacob set the page on the desk.

The air shifted.

A low vibration moved through the floor—a quiet resonance, like a room breathing in reverse. Hem pinged sharply.

"Audio resonance activated. Passive signal released.
Trace detected—external response initiated."

Nex's voice sharpened.

"Signal not isolated. Interference signature triangulated.
Response from Bucharest."

Jacob's head snapped toward Hannah. "Leyla?"

Nex did not answer.

And the room, holding its breath.

The silence fractured.

A sound—barely audible, like a sigh through the walls—followed by a soft, rhythmic tap. Not the wind. Not the monastery. Something else.

Hannah looked at Jacob. "That wasn't the building."

Jacob raised a hand. "Hem, re-scan the perimeter."

Hem's voice sharpened.

"New movement detected. Above-ground corridor. Human-sized thermal signature. Stationary, west stairwell landing. Duration: 43 seconds."

Nex followed immediately.

"Residual digital pulse detected. Unregistered device attempted handshake with local mesh. Failed. Origin: unknown."

Jacob's jaw tightened. "We're not alone down here."

Hannah reached for the cloth bundle and Ethan's note. "We move. Now."

They doused the torch and began the ascent, careful but fast. The steps felt steeper this time—like the monastery wanted to hold them back. The silence no longer carried reverence. It carried risk.

Reaching the gate, Jacob paused only long enough to secure the latch behind them. No alarms. No footsteps. Whoever had been there wasn't following—but they had been watching.

They emerged into night.

The monastery courtyard was mostly empty now, blanketed in blue dusk and falling mist. Somewhere overhead, the bells gave a final, muted chime. No one lingered. The crows were gone.

At the far end of the block, the tramline buzzed faintly to life, headlights slicing through mist as the next tram rumbled around the corner—vintage silver-blue, its frame humming like an old radio.

Jacob grabbed Hannah's elbow. "Tram. Let's move."

They boarded just as the doors hissed shut behind them. The tram rocked gently as it pulled away from the monastery gate and slid into the arteries of the old city.

The interior was a blend of old brass fittings and scratched windows—a holdover from the Cold War era, now upgraded with contactless passes and quiet electric glide. Iași's trams were more than transport—they were connective tissue, bridging old neighborhoods, university districts, and working-class corners of the city.

As the tram curved downhill toward the city centre, shopfronts flickered by: used bookstores, bakeries with still-warm glass, art galleries set into tiled facades. Elderly passengers sat beside students with earbuds and books open across their knees.

Jacob watched Hannah out of the corner of his eye. Her face was unreadable—focused, steady, present.

He looked at her—not as the analyst or the strategist—but as his little sister. The one who used to follow him barefoot down riverbanks, even when she was scared. The one who always asked the harder questions. He remembered Ethan calling her "the anchor" once, in a half-laugh, half-warning—saying she was the one who could hold people without asking to be held in return.

Now, she sat across from him with half the map to a forgotten legacy tucked beneath her jacket, and not a flicker of doubt in her eyes. Jacob felt something hard press against the space just under his ribs. It wasn't pride. It was something older—remorse. For not protecting her. For not believing in her sooner.

He turned to the window, cleared his throat.

The tram slowed. They stepped off near Piața Unirii, the heart of the city—the old Ottoman trading square had changed names over centuries, but not its rhythm: now lined with bars, late cafés, families gathering under market awnings and bookstores whose windows glowed with filament bulbs and philosophy volumes.

"Food?" Hannah asked, without breaking stride.

"Yeah," Jacob said. "Hem's running a scan sweep in the background, all clear for now."

They crossed into a small side street where a line had formed beside a kürtőskalács stand, its chimney cakes steaming over charcoal, and beside it, a man grilled mititei—spiced meat rolls—over a barrel lid covered in foil.

They ate standing beneath an awning while mist rolled off the tramlines.

The city moved around them: couples passing beneath coats, students speaking three languages in one sentence, a violinist playing something soft and ancient just across the street. Someone's dog barked, leash tangled in café chairs. Above, wind chimes played softly from a balcony garden strung with orange lights.

Hannah said nothing at first, just tore a piece of bread and handed Jacob his half.

He accepted it. "You okay?"

She nodded. "Ethan once told me this city sang even when no one was listening. I think he was right."

Jacob chewed, eyes scanning their perimeter. "Still quiet. Hem?"

"No anomalies within 500-metre radius. Tracking local mesh for passive pings."

For a moment, they were just two siblings with street food, standing in a city that remembered too much and said too little.

"Do you think Leyla's in Istanbul?" Hannah spoke breaking the silence.

Jacob chewed, nodded once. "She always returns to the beginning. Even when she says she's done with it."

Hem pinged.

"Room integrity breached. Entry timestamp: 18 minutes ago. Motion recorded. Internal microphone offline. Visual sensor—compromised."

Jacob's voice dropped. "Let's get back. Quietly."

Later, they returned to the inn on foot, sticking to smaller roads and alleys while observing Iasi by night. Shops getting busier and the hum of television static drifted from upstairs windows. A couple argued gently in Romanian on a stoop. The night folded inward as they approached the inn.

By the time they arrived, the lobby was empty. The night clerk was asleep behind a tattered paperback, must be a rather boring book. The lights were dim in the stairwell.

They moved quickly, quietly, up to the second floor.

Jacob unlocked their door.

The lights were off. The curtains undisturbed.

Everything looked untouched.

But it wasn't.

The drawer where Hannah had tucked away Ethan's note—the original one, from Iasi—was open. The letter was gone.

The one piece of Ethan's handwriting they hadn't copied.

Jacob scanned the room slowly. "They took it."

On the bed, placed carefully atop the turned-down cover: a matchbook.

Hannah opened it.

"You're not the only ones listening."

Hem buzzed again.

"Signal review complete. Secondary Cedrela variation detected. Timestamp: two days prior. Location:

115

Istanbul. Source classification—unverified. Confidence threshold: 72% match with Project Lale cipher."

Nex's tone turned opaque.

"Leyla's involvement cannot be ruled out. Likelihood of planted misdirection: increasing."

Jacob stepped to the window, stared into the dark.

"She's either warning us," he said, "or someone's using her shadow."

Hannah folded Ethan's second letter carefully, as though by holding what was left, she could delay the moment it became a memory.

"Then we go to the place where he built the first map."

Jacob turned to her, already knowing the answer.

"Istanbul," she said.

And behind them, the room stood still—no longer safe, no longer theirs.

"He didn't leave a trail," Hannah whispered. "He left a gauntlet."

—Some things don't fade. They wait.

Chapter Thirteen - The First Map

Jacob stood by the inn's window in Iași, the morning grey with low cloud and sleep-heavy silence. Hannah was at the desk, zipping the last of their bags. The air between them held something tight—unspoken, but present.

"Check-out's too quiet," Jacob muttered.

Hannah glanced at the hallway. "We don't linger."

They descended the stairs with controlled urgency. At reception, the clerk smiled too long. Jacob didn't smile back. He placed cash on the counter, not a card.

Outside, mist curled around the car Hem had arranged—plain grey, plates registered to a dissolved Moldovan logistics firm.

"Next leg arranged," Hem reported in Jacob's earpiece.

"Depart Iași airfield via charter. Stopover through Constanța. Arrive Istanbul pre-dusk. Rental vehicle will meet you at Gate D, Sabiha Gökçen. Lodging verified and secured."

As the car pulled into the main road, Jacob looked over his shoulder once. The inn's curtains didn't move. The street remained still.

Iași Regional Airport was modest—a Cold War-era holdover now flanked by low terminals and construction scaffolding. It served mostly domestic flights, student traffic, and seasonal tourism. But this morning, the tarmac was unusually bare. Their charter was already waiting.

Inside the terminal, Jacob said, "You sure no one's shadowing us?"

Hem answered dryly.

"If they are, they're better than me."

As the plane began its descent into Istanbul, Hannah pressed her forehead against the window. The city unfurled beneath her—not like a map, but like a memory pulled loose.

The Bosphorus curved like a ribbon of ink across the page, split between continents and intentions. Golden domes shimmered like molten punctuation marks. The Blue Mosque, Hagia Sophia, and the worn serpentine spine of the ancient city walls appeared in silhouette.

Once, these walls had divided emperors from their assassins.

Now, traffic streamed beside them like modern processions—no less desperate, only quieter.

She remembered what Ethan had once said, watching the city from a ferry:

"Istanbul doesn't rise. It lingers."

It still did.

Jacob took in Sabiha Gökçen Airport like a strategist: long terminals, high glass walls, too much space for comfort.

"Efficient," he muttered. "But it listens too well."

At Immigration and security clearance, Hannah scanned the faces of staff and passengers. Nothing out of place, but her pulse ticked harder anyway.

Nex chimed softly.

"Frequency lock updated, Mesh scrubbed. Device shadow signatures removed. Communication line clear."

Hem added,
"Local data pings erased post-checkpoint. Istanbul ready."
Hem chimed in as soon as both of them cleared immigration and customs.

"Vehicle waiting. No visual anomalies on exterior approach. Driver ID verified and anonymised."

The valet met them as instructed. No signage. No small talk. Just a nod as he handed Jacob the keys—standard black fob, unbranded. Jacob returned the nod, already reading the car's dimensions by touch.

No luggage assistance. No names.

Just movement.

The vehicle merged smoothly onto the motorway. By mid to late morning, Istanbul had gathered around them—raw and sprawling, a city you didn't enter so much as dissolve into.

As they crossed into Fatih, Hannah spoke without being asked:

"Named after Mehmed II. The Conqueror. Once the Byzantine religious seat. Then the Ottoman nerve centre for 470 years. Twenty-five percent of the city's protected architecture lives here. This is where history keeps breathing."

She was almost whispering by the end.

Hannah looked out at the passing façades—arched windows, brass knockers, ancient brickwork streaked with shadow. Minarets stood beside satellite dishes. A pharmacy shared a wall with a 17th-century spice shop.

"Everything's layered," she said.

Jacob replied, "Like it's all still listening."

Their destination was the Romance Istanbul Hotel, a discreet boutique inn known more for its preservationist design than its press coverage. It had once been an Ottoman home—wood-beamed, tiled, with three floors and a hidden courtyard. Today, it stood as a quiet remnant just off Sultanahmet Square, a minute's walk from Gülhane Park and the gates of Topkapı Palace.

The square outside was hushed with the wind off the Bosphorus. In the Ottoman era, it had been the stage for imperial decrees, Janissary marches, and exile lists announced in whispers. Now it pulsed with tourists and street vendors—but in twilight, it returned to silence.

At reception, they paid in cash. No registration under their real names.

As they reached the second floor, Jacob paused at the room. "Hem?"

"Room clear. No electromagnetic residue. No thermal variance. Clean entry."

Jacob unlocked the door.

The room opened in blues and brass. Two single beds. Heavy velvet curtains. Woven carpets in deep crimsons and navy, its centre medallion shaped like a tulip swallowed by flame and a writing desk carved with tulip motifs. The walls bore framed sketches of 19th-century Istanbul—when steamships lined the Golden Horn and spies prayed beside scholars in every teahouse.

The air smelled faintly of rosewater and cedar.

Hannah tossed her bag onto the nearest bed and sat down slowly, hands resting in her lap.

Jacob looked around, then spoke first. "What do you remember about it? The palace."

Hannah didn't look up. "Not the grandeur. The cruelty."

FLASHBACK

Ethan, years ago, pacing before the miniature model of Topkapı Palace he'd built in their apartment—matchsticks for columns, copper wire for domes.

"They called it the Golden Cage. The Kafes. That's where they kept the princes—their brothers, cousins, uncles. So they wouldn't have to be murdered outright. Just... contained. Until they either lost their mind or accepted the silence."

He had tapped one corner of the model: the privy chamber, where execution orders were signed.

"Prince Mustafa was strangled in that room. Suleiman's son. Ordered by Roxelana—Hürrem Sultan—through whispers to protect her own."

Ethan paused, his voice quieter.

"The empire didn't collapse from war, Han. It collapsed from memory management. Cedrela didn't start as a code. It started as a rebellion against forgetting."

Hannah opened her eyes. "Ethan wasn't obsessed with legacy. He was terrified of it."

Jacob sat across from her. "Then let's find what terrified him most."

They left the hotel just as the muezzin's call folded into twilight.

Istanbul by dusk was a spell half-cast—lanterns flickered awake along the lanes of Sultanahmet, and the scent of roasted chestnuts drifted across the square. The air was thick with stories. The kind you didn't read. The kind you overheard.

Hannah and Jacob walked without speaking at first, each step echoing on centuries of stone.

Around them, history moved with casual grace:

—The Obelisk of Theodosius, once dragged from Karnak under Roman command.

—The Hagia Sophia, which had changed gods more times than it had cracked tiles.

—And the Basilica Cistern, hidden beneath them, still whispering its water-born secrets in the dark.

"This square," Hannah murmured, "has witnessed emperors crowned, Janissaries revolting, and poets hanged. All in the same hundred yards."

Jacob offered a low whistle.

She continued, gesturing to the skyline beyond the tea vendors. "And Topkapı watched it all."

They turned down a quieter street where a vintage clothier glowed warm from within. Inside, worn jackets and linen shirts hung on iron racks. Jacob found a sand-coloured coat that fit. Hannah grabbed a navy jumper and a long charcoal scarf.

As they paid, Hem chimed in softly.

"Local facial scans consistent with non-persistent traffic.
No trace logs detected. Surveillance levels low. Network chatter below threshold. Clean."

Back outside, they picked up kebabs and sweet tea from a corner stall and walked along the perimeter of Gülhane Park. Beyond the trees, Topkapı's outline grew sharper.

Its silhouette wasn't just regal. It was unforgiving.

Columns lifted high above the pavilions like sentinels. The Gate of Felicity, gleaming even in dusk, had once been the backdrop for executions signed in silence.

"This place..." Hannah breathed.

"Like the Taj Mahal," Jacob said. "Beautiful. And built on grief."

She nodded. "And like the Kremlin. Versailles. The Forbidden City. Power never builds quietly."

Back in their room, the air felt heavier than before—like the city had followed them home.

Jacob sat at the edge of his bed, polishing his watch. Hannah stood by the window, Topkapı glowing in the fog.

He's still here, she thought. Not his body. His argument.

She turned. "Jacob?"

He looked up.

"If something happens tomorrow... I want you to know—Ethan didn't trust many people. But he trusted you. Even when you disappeared."

Jacob didn't speak. But something behind his eyes shifted.

They left the hotel just after sunrise, weaving through Sultanahmet's stone-paved streets as the city exhaled into morning. The air was cool, touched with the tang of salt and brewing tea. From every rooftop came the faint sound of cooing doves and early prayer.

Hannah led without speaking.

They passed closed souvenir shops and sleeping cats curled under benches. A boy pushed a cart of simit across the square. The old city was still half in dream.

Topkapı rose through the morning mist like it remembered too much. The gates opened without question—Hem had seeded their credentials into the temporary guest list of an archival digitisation project. Nex scrubbed their data trail in real time.

As they approached the Imperial Gate, Hannah slowed again.

Topkapı was breathtaking.

The Gate of Salutation rose in pale stone and delicate calligraphy, flanked by battlements that caught light like sculpture. The domes beyond gleamed like eggshells dipped in fire. In the open courts, shadows stretched like prayers.

But beauty, Hannah knew, had a price.

Behind that beauty had lived poisoners, whisperers, and mourners. Eunuchs who had burned secrets. Sultanas who orchestrated wars. Daughters who had died unnamed but changed dynasties.

They approached not through the main gate, but through the lesser-known Gate of the Harem, as marked in Ethan's notes—"They don't guard what they forget."

At the gate, Jacob flashed the laminated passes Hem had generated overnight—archivist credentials cross-linked with a defunct restoration project.

The guard scanned them once, shrugged, and waved them through.

Inside, the palace felt weightless in its silence. Arched corridors lined with Iznik tiles glowed faintly in the early light. The Courtyard of the Concubines whispered of velvet and politics. The Imperial Hall, though empty, still felt full of memory.

In the Harem, Hannah paused before a painted doorway.

"Valide Sultan's chambers," she whispered. "The private domain of the sultan's mother—once the most powerful woman in the empire. This was her throne room. Without a throne."

Jacob said nothing. He just watched her.

The farther they walked, the more the palace felt like a living system—labyrinthine, breathing in the absence of its former keepers.

They descended into the archival wing, tucked behind the kitchens. The corridor narrowed, lit only by sporadic bulbs and daylight filtering through oculi above.

Plastic sheeting covered shelving units. Dust floated in the air like ghosted signatures.

"Ethan said this was the heart," Hannah whispered. "The place where Cedrela was born in metaphor."

FLASHBACK

Ethan, sitting cross-legged on a ferry, Istanbul behind him. A notebook balanced on one knee.

"Cedrela isn't just memory. It's the resistance to curated memory. To what empires want us to forget."

He tapped a page—an aerial layout of Topkapı.

"They didn't just kill people here, Han. They erased the echo."

In the archival wing, the halls narrowed. Shelving units draped in plastic. The silence changed here—thicker, intentional.

Hem pinged.

"Object identified. Row three. Compartment 12-B. Parchment. Encoding signature: Goldstein. Variant: Pre-structural Cedrela."

Nex followed.

"Caution. Secondary signature detected nearby. Unfamiliar construct. Possible trail or bait."

Jacob placed a hand on Hannah's arm. "I'll keep watch."

She nodded and stepped toward the canvas map mounted on the shelf. Behind it: a small drawer.

She slid it open slowly.

The parchment crackled softly beneath her fingertips, like it didn't want to be held.

Inside: a single page of parchment, musical symbols swirling outward like a rose in ink. Not linear. Not even a melody.

"This isn't a score," she murmured. "It's a directive."

Nex whispered:

"Fragment: 'First Map'. Activation: dormant. Signal: emotional memory trigger pending."

Then Hem flared red.

"Movement. South corridor. Unsanctioned pass. Speed: 3.4 metres/second. Closing."

Jacob drew her back. They pressed into the shadows.

A shape moved past the aisle—a man in custodial overalls. But he didn't glance side to side. Didn't push a cart. No ID badge.

Hem's voice was low.

"Biometric mismatch. Not staff. Not visitor."

The man stopped at the map display.

Paused.

Then kept walking.

Hannah exhaled shakily. "He wasn't looking for something."

Jacob replied, "He was checking to see if someone had found it."

Inside the drawer, beneath the parchment, lay a second clue—a broken chain with a locket.

Hannah opened it gently. Inside: a thumbnail image of a tulip. Inlaid with Ottoman script:

"Truth outlasts obedience."

She held it carefully, and for a moment, remembered a childhood spring: Ethan pressing a tulip petal into her journal.

"They're just flowers," she'd said.

"Not always," he'd replied.

Back at the hotel that night, Hannah lay on the bed, staring at the ceiling. Jacob was already asleep, one arm over his face, his breathing slow.

The city outside still hadn't quieted.

In the shadows, she replayed Ethan's voice, the lines in his notebook, the tiny spaces between his silence.

He didn't want to be remembered. He wanted us to remember something else.

And now she knew what Cedrela really was.

Not a cipher.

A confrontation.

The silence didn't leave when they returned to the hotel.

It came with them—folded into Hannah's scarf, clinging to the scent of parchment and old dust from Topkapı's archives. The locket lay open on the nightstand now, its tulip glinting faintly in the amber light. Outside, Istanbul continued humming—a lullaby of horns, heels on stone, and muezzin echoes dissolving into night.

Jacob stood at the window, tracking movement below. Hannah sat curled on the edge of her bed, staring at nothing. She hadn't said a word since they left the palace. She didn't need to.

Hem broke the stillness.

"Unregistered signal detected. Localised spike in encrypted Cedrela-variant packet transmission. Origin: intra-building."

Jacob's voice was quiet. "How close?"

"Very. Signal proximity suggests within five metres. Possibly adjacent room."

Nex followed, his tone unusually reserved.

"Partial decryption engaged. Audio fragment: Ethan. Authentic, though degraded. Playback commencing."

A hush. Then—

"...you have to listen backwards. Cedrela was never about what's played... it's what's withheld... the silence contains the weight..."

The voice collapsed into a burst of static, like a transmission dissolving mid-thought.

Hannah sat up slowly. Her breath was shallow. "That wasn't a file," she murmured. "It was a relay. Someone's playing fragments like they're... testing him."

Jacob was already moving. "Or us."

He crossed to the shared wall and pressed his palm flat against it. It was cool—undisturbed. Hem scanned it silently.

"No acoustic bleed. Signal not from neighbouring suite. Broadcast was hyper-local. Device signal self-terminated. Fragment encoded to expire post-transmission."

Nex chimed in—quieter than before.

"This wasn't stored. It was designed to be heard once. It's an echo."

Hannah stood, the locket now clutched in her hand. "Then someone's playing Ethan like he's a memory file."

Jacob looked at her, jaw clenched. "Or trying to see what still speaks."

They didn't linger.

Jacob led them down the back stairwell and out through the service corridor. The alley behind the hotel smelled of damp stone and cigarette ash. A street cat blinked at them from atop a crate and vanished.

They moved without speaking, past a shuttered spice stall and an iron-grated bookshop. Jacob didn't like the way the street breathed tonight—too quiet where it should've been noisy. Too still where it should've moved.

Hem pulsed again.

"New location tag embedded in Cedrela metadata fragment. Visual reference match: Süleymaniye Library."

Hannah looked up sharply. "That was his escape hatch. Whenever he didn't want to be found."

Nex followed.

"Secondary fragment unlocked from drawer scan. Image embedded in locket chain."

Jacob's smartglass blinked. An image unfolded—Ethan, standing in a cramped, paper-filled room. The lighting was low, but his eyes were lit with intent. He wasn't looking at the camera. He was talking to someone just out of frame.

Jacob zoomed in.

There. In the far corner.

A shoulder. A jawline. Part of a coat. The shape of a man.

And something flickered in Jacob's eyes—recognition, or a ghost of it.

"He said he was dead," Jacob whispered. "But he's not."

—He carried it here.

Chapter Fourteen - The Library of Echoes

The Süleymaniye Library didn't look like a library. It looked like memory carved into stone.

Set just behind the great mosque complex of Süleymaniye, the building rested high above the Bosphorus like a sentinel, its pale stone walls streaked with light and history. Arched windows lined its southern façade. Minaret shadows slid slowly across its tiled roof. The entrance—a modest arch flanked by calligraphy panels—opened into silence that felt rehearsed.

"It was built in 1557," Hannah said as they approached. "By Sinan, the imperial architect. Part of Suleiman's vision to make knowledge a pillar of power."

Jacob raised an eyebrow. "A sanctuary for scholars?"

Hannah nodded. "And for state control. Every manuscript that passed through here was copied. Reviewed. Coded. It was beautiful... and watched."

As they passed through the archway, her steps slowed.

She had come here before. Alone, and once with Ethan. He'd brought her to see a rare map of the Levant, but they hadn't looked at maps. They'd talked for hours in the theology section—about ideas that outlived their empires.

Now the space felt different.

Hollowed.

They crossed the vestibule, entered the main hall. Domes curved gently overhead, painted in soft blues and gold. Slender columns separated alcoves filled with manuscripts, catalogues, digital terminals. The scent of old paper and lemon-oil polish lingered.

Hannah and Jacob approached it at a careful pace.

"This is where he came to disappear," she said softly, pulling her coat closer. "He called it the quietest room in Istanbul."

Jacob scanned the building. "Quiet's not always safe."

Hem pinged into Jacob's ear.

"Restoration credentials accepted. No flagged identities present. Cedrela echo trace detected. Sub-archive vault. Timestamp matches Goldstein log: eighteen months prior."

Jacob glanced at Hannah. "He was here. Same day Nex lost track of him."

It had been almost a week since Ethan vanished—days spent chasing echoes, crossing borders, trying to stay ahead of shadows they couldn't quite name.

She didn't speak. She just moved.

They crossed the threshold beneath a low, domed vestibule. Inside, the world softened—domes curved like the inside of a shell, calligraphic panels caught the dusk light, and silence didn't feel imposed; it felt inherited.

Rows of researchers sat at long wooden tables. Lamps cast golden halos over manuscripts, laptops, ink-stained fingertips. The smell of parchment, tea, and electricity mingled in a way only Istanbul could balance.

The stairs to the vault were unmarked—stone steps behind a lacquered panel that once held Ottoman court poetry. They descended slowly, each footfall swallowed by the thick silence below.

At the base of the stairwell, a small antechamber. Iron gate. No camera.

Hem spoke again.

> "Mechanical lock ahead. No surveillance grid in place. Biometric scanner nonfunctional. Physical override possible."

Jacob pulled the gate open with a slow groan of rusted hinges. They stepped into the sealed reading room.

It was cold. The kind of cold that preserved things long dead.

Books lay untouched in latticed cupboards. The walls bore nothing but faded tulip motifs painted directly onto the stone. And near the center, a single desk beneath a domed oculus.

"This is where he sat," Hannah said, her voice a breath. "Ethan always said Süleymaniye held the echoes longer than anywhere else."

A linen-wrapped folio sat at the desk. She approached, fingertips grazing its edge. The wax seal had been broken before.

Inside: pages of Ottoman theological theory and legal philosophy. In the margins—Ethan's hand, marking translation notes in English and red tulip stamps beside select phrases.

One of the final pages was different—modern paper, thinner, hand-folded once.

Hannah opened it.

The Cedrela spiral unfolded—delicate, like a map of grief.

Nex chimed in Jacob's ear.

"Match confirmed. Variant-3 Cedrela cipher. Memory pattern incomplete. Echo-based trigger suspected."

Then Jacob froze.

A sound—subtle. A shift in weight. A creak of something human and patient.

Hem's voice came tight.

"Acoustic disturbance. North corridor. Single subject. Still. No pattern of retreat."

Jacob whispered: "There's someone listening."

Hannah looked at him, tense. "They're not moving?"

Jacob shook his head. "Not yet."

He stepped slowly toward the wall. The stone absorbed sound like water.

Then—

A brief scuff. A shoe on polished floor.

Jacob moved back to Hannah. "Tuck it away. Now."

She slipped the spiral into her coat. Then paused. Her gaze had caught something etched into the far wall behind the desk—barely visible.

A tulip, again. But smaller. Older.

Beneath it, an inscription in Ottoman Turkish.

Nex translated quietly:

"Memory is obedience's enemy."

Jacob whispered, "There's more."

Nex again:

"Trace chemical compound identified. Pollen, resin, and ambient particulates... consistent with materials catalogued at Vienna Archive. Date exposure: post-Goldstein disappearance."

Jacob's chest tightened.

"We're not chasing Ethan," he said. "We're walking someone else's trail. His, maybe. Or someone who got there after."

He looked toward the corridor—where the sound had come from.

The silence hadn't returned.

It had shifted.

And it was listening back.

They didn't speak as they stepped deeper into the vault.

The stone corridor narrowed, the air pressing inward, sharp with the scent of limestone, oil, and age. Jacob's torch cast thin shadows onto the walls, where geometric designs curled like sleeping scripts.

At the far end of the passage, a narrow brass grate broke the otherwise unbroken masonry. It looked like a defunct heating vent, set just above eye level.

But Hem pinged softly.

"Unregistered resonance signature detected. Embedded Cedrela pattern—non-musical. Visual key structure present."

Jacob stepped forward, tracing the grill with his fingertips. "It's not airflow," he murmured. "It's a lock."

Hannah raised an eyebrow. "He hid a vault inside a library vault?"

Jacob pointed to a series of tulip motifs etched into the brass filigree—three of them marked faintly with red pigment. Ethan's red.

Confirmation from Hem followed;

> "Cross-reference activated, match found: annotation from theological manuscript—page twelve, third line. Correlation matrix identified. Cipher integrity at eighty-four percent."

Jacob turned back toward the reading room and returned with the folio.

Together, they aligned the motifs, following the annotations like a score. On the final press, the grate clicked—and swung outward.

Behind it: a small, recessed chamber, no larger than a confession booth. Its interior was lined in cedar and filled with shelves—rows of leather-bound codices, untouched by light.

"This wasn't just hidden," Hannah whispered. "It was never meant to be found by accident."

Jacob stepped in first, eyes sweeping the tight space.

Most of the volumes were old—some older than the Republic itself. Subjects ranged from legal reform under Sultan Abdulhamid II, particularly his obsession with loyalty oaths and censorship, to mystic writings on divine memory and poetic resistance that had been banned during the Tanzimat era. Titles were embossed in fading gold:

- On the Shadow of Caliphate

- Al-Mazmūn wa'l-Sirr (The Allegory and the Secret)

- The Doctrine of Speechless Justice

These weren't just books. They were dangerous thoughts with bindings.

But one stood out—mid-shelf, centre, newer binding. A strip of white paper marked it, bearing a single Ottoman word:

"Divanül-Kitāb."
The Book within the Books.

Jacob opened it with care. Pages crackled. The scent of pressed silk and rosewater rose from within.

Near the centre: a folded page. Modern. Unbound. He unfolded it slowly, heart already knowing.

A letter. Addressed not to Hannah.

To him.

"Jacob,"

If you're reading this, it means I've either failed, or succeeded in a way that made me silent.

You always saw things in straight lines. I envied that. Cedrela doesn't move in straight lines. It spirals. Like memory. Like guilt.

There's something beneath the code. It's not just music. It's intent. And if that intent is ever replicated without context, it becomes a weapon.

You'll want to follow it. But ask yourself—are you protecting truth, or chasing something that will unmake it?

We weren't meant to finish this. We were meant to guard it until it faded.

Don't trust the shape of silence. Even mine.

—O

There was no name. Only a red tulip, drawn in a stroke Jacob recognised. And a symbol beneath it—an angular glyph Nex couldn't decrypt.

A sudden chill moved through the room—like a held breath released. Jacob flinched slightly.

The air had changed.

Like they had tripped a silent wire.

Hannah read it over his shoulder. "He wrote this for you."

Jacob folded the letter once. "He warned me."

Her voice cracked. "He never doubted you."

Jacob didn't answer right away. He stared at the tulip.

"Maybe he should have."

They returned the book to the shelf. But as Jacob closed the cover, Hem flared red.

"New data signature detected. Tracking beacon embedded in spine adhesive. Non-Ethan origin. Timestamp: post-Goldstein disappearance."

Nex pulsed once. Then again.

"Digital watermark detected. Signature metadata: M.Orman_ΔΞ–1."

Jacob blinked.

Then very softly, almost to himself, he said, "Mehmet."

Hannah looked at him sharply. "What?"

Jacob looked back once toward the sealed chamber—toward the tulip, the scent, the fear in Ethan's unfinished warning.

Then he stepped into the corridor, the shadows curling like script behind him.

The door to the sealed vault clicked shut behind them.

Hannah and Jacob stood still for a moment in the quiet corridor outside the archive. The light here was different—cooler, thinner, like history had exhaled around them.

"I hate how calm it looks now," Hannah murmured.

Jacob didn't answer. His posture had shifted—watchful, alert, spine drawn taut.

They didn't return through the main reading room. Hem had pinged a lesser-known exit—through the back courtyard that once held the Ottoman water clock, commissioned by Sultan Ahmed III and engineered by Mehmed Çelebi. A marvel of its time, the clock had used floating bowls and timed levers to mark both prayer cycles and imperial shifts.

Now, only the bones remained: the basin half-cracked, bronze pipework oxidised to green, time stilled mid-thought.

As they passed it, Hannah slowed, her breath catching slightly.

"I remember Ethan explaining how it worked," she said quietly. "I didn't understand most of it... but he said it was the one clock that didn't tick—it flowed. Like memory. Like time should."

She smiled faintly, just for a breath.

"Jacob was always trying to fix the mechanical ones. Ethan wanted to hear how they failed."

They passed shuttered restoration rooms, small prayer alcoves still rich with the scent of wax and old cedar. The air grew cooler. Stone steps spiralled upward, uneven from centuries of breathless passage.

And for a moment—just a flicker—Hannah remembered the three of them racing up a different stairwell, Jacob two steps ahead, Ethan narrating something poetic just to annoy them.

Near the top of the stairwell's curve, Jacob paused. A line of Ottoman script was scratched into a marble sill:

"Obedience listens. Truth echoes."

They both stared.

"Feels like something he would've left," Hannah whispered.

Jacob ran his thumb over it. "Or something left for him."

As they stepped into the final courtyard, dusk had darkened into slate blue. Floodlights caught the minarets in angled beams, cutting sharp lines across the ancient façade.

Nex pulsed in Jacob's ear.

"Repeating pulse signature detected. Originating across four museum nodes. Encryption matches Cedrela substructure. Five-second delay loop active."

Jacob frowned. "You're saying someone's pinging the system?"

"They're baiting Cedrela fragments—broadcasting echoes to test for sentient response."

"Like sonar for ghosts," Jacob muttered.

Nex confirmed.

"Target unknown. Signature consistent with digital sonar logic. Purpose: to trigger latent Cedrela responses."

"Mehmet," Jacob said. "He's sending pieces. Not to us. To the network."

They reached the outer courtyard—silent, windless. And there, exactly fifteen metres ahead, at the base of a column fractured along its spine, a lone figure stood. Long coat. Shoulders square. Face obscured beneath a dark brimmed cap.

He didn't speak.

He simply bent—deliberate, smooth—and placed a folded parchment onto the stone. Then straightened. Turned.

And walked away.

Not fast. But sure.

Jacob stepped forward. "Hey!"

The man didn't flinch.

By the time Jacob reached the column, the figure had slipped past the arch and vanished into the alley beyond. Gone like steam over stone.

Hannah crouched and picked up the parchment. It trembled slightly in her fingers.

A hand-drawn map of Istanbul, annotated in a style they both knew.

Ethan's.

But the ink hadn't dried fully.

Nex pinged again.

"Ink composition non-archival. Paper fibre contact timestamp: 42 minutes prior. Heat transfer still active."

Jacob said, low and flat, "He carried it here."
Nex pulsed again—sharper this time.

"Breath trace confirmed. Voice subharmonics logged during passage. Partial biometric correlation: Ethan Goldstein. Confidence threshold: 82%."

Hannah froze.
She didn't look at Jacob. She couldn't.
The weight of it collapsed through her like a hidden floor giving way. 82% wasn't certainty—but it wasn't a lie either. It was just enough to let hope in. Just enough to weaponise it.
What if it was him?
What if it wasn't?
Her voice stuck in her throat.
Jacob touched her shoulder gently.
"He wouldn't just watch us like this," she whispered.
Jacob's voice was low. "Maybe he didn't have a choice."
She finally looked up.
Her pulse kicked. Her throat tightened, as if the air had become too thick to pull through.
Her fingers tightened around the parchment. "That voice... that breath. If he's alive—why this? Why stay a ghost?"
Her gaze fixed on the column, on the place where shadow met stone. On the space where he had stood.
Everything inside her fought to keep her standing still.
Then she spoke, barely above a whisper.

—"Whatever Ethan started," Hannah said, "we're not the only ones trying to finish it."

Chapter Fifteen - The Ritual in Tbilisi

Jacob stood at the hotel window in Istanbul, murmuring quiet instructions to Hem. "We need everything clean—passports, flight manifests, tickets. Route us through something neutral. Use the names we've stored for emergencies."

Hem replied instantly, crisp and efficient.

> "Confirmed. Passports under alternate identities secured. Departure via Istanbul Airport, arriving in Tbilisi, Georgia. Rental car arranged at Tbilisi International, under alias."

Behind Jacob, Hannah sat silently at the edge of the bed, half-listening, her fingertips gently tracing Ethan's worn notebook. She felt its warmth, the softness of its aged leather against her skin. In that quiet, tension-filled moment, memories surfaced with tender clarity.

FLASHBACK

She stood with Ethan years earlier, overlooking Istanbul from Galata Tower. Twilight had spread across the Bosphorus, lights flickering to life like distant fireflies. Ethan's voice was soft yet vividly alive beside her.

"You know, every city has a hidden melody, Han," he had said, a gentle smile forming at the corners of his eyes. "You can't hear it with your ears. You have to feel it in your bones."

She remembered her quiet laughter, a soft skepticism blending with admiration. "That sounds like something you'd say in class to impress your students."

He'd chuckled, shaking his head gently. "No, it's real. Each place holds memories in its streets, its buildings, in the way people glance at each other when they think no one notices. Listen closely enough, and you'll feel centuries in seconds."

His gaze had turned serious then, searching her face softly in the evening shadows. "Promise me you'll never stop listening, Hannah—not even when it's painful."

The ache of his absence had never felt sharper than now. But sitting on the bed, watching Jacob carefully plan their survival, Hannah realized Ethan hadn't left only memories behind. He'd left her his strength, his curiosity, his defiance. She straightened her shoulders and took a deep, calming breath. She would carry his voice with her, even now, into whatever waited in Tbilisi.

Jacob's voice gently drew her back. "We're ready. Are you?"

She lifted her chin, meeting his eyes. "Yes. Let's finish this."

As their flight descended toward Tbilisi, the city appeared below, glittering softly in twilight—a constellation nestled between rugged hills and the dark ribbon of the Kura River. Tbilisi was vibrant yet mysterious, a place suspended between its Ottoman past and modern complexities.

Jacob gazed thoughtfully out the window. "Tbilisi's strategic. Close enough politically and economically tied to Turkey to matter, yet independent enough to stay beyond Mehmet's immediate reach."

Hannah nodded, recalling Ethan's notes: during Ottoman rule, Tbilisi had been a city of crossroads, battles, and cautious diplomacy. Now it stood independent, ambitious yet shadowed by its complex history—an echo of past empires balanced precariously on the edge of a new identity.

Jacob shifted slightly, catching the hint of sorrow in her reflection. "Han, you okay?"

She turned slowly toward him, her gaze softening as she met his eyes. "Do you remember that summer we went camping near Lake Van? You and Ethan argued about history and politics until sunrise."

A gentle, almost shy smile crossed Jacob's face. "And you spent the whole night telling us both we were hopeless."

Her laugh was soft and warm, the sound catching in her throat. "I loved that night. Ethan was always the thinker, but you—you were always his compass, Jake. He trusted your instincts, even when he challenged them."

Jacob's voice softened, nearly inaudible over the drone of the engines. "And now?"

She reached out gently, squeezing his hand. "He would be proud of you. And grateful, just like I am."

Jacob's expression held steady, though his eyes revealed a brief shimmer of vulnerability. "You know, Hannah, he worried about protecting you most. But it's you who's protected both of us. All along."

Silence fell between them, warm and comfortable, a quiet bridge rebuilding something nearly lost.

They landed quietly, slipping through customs seamlessly with identities Hem had prepared. Outside, the rental car awaited—an unremarkable sedan, its license plates neatly anonymized.

As Jacob navigated from the airport into the heart of Tbilisi, the city unveiled itself in quiet fragments. Narrow streets twisted gently between buildings of crumbling elegance, their facades painted shades of amber, mustard, and rust. Ancient wooden balconies draped in ivy and delicate latticework seemed to whisper their Georgian secrets in the gathering dusk.

Jacob spoke softly as he drove, Hem murmuring quiet directions in his ear. "This place was Ottoman once—powerful, but uneasy. Now it's finding its footing again, caught between East and West, history and ambition."

She watched quietly through the window, captivated by glimpses of old stone churches, quaint cafes glowing warmly, and ancient walls etched with Georgian script. A city comfortable with contradiction—beauty in decay, strength in vulnerability.

They checked into the Tiflis Palace, a hotel Hem had carefully selected, perched high above the Kura River near the historic Metekhi district. Built over a century earlier, its walls remembered revolutions, poetry, and whispered secrets. Ornate Georgian architecture blended with Art Nouveau touches, each corridor and room steeped in memories of diplomats, artists, and spies.

Inside their room, Hannah allowed herself only a brief moment of rest—washing the travel away, changing swiftly into neutral tones. Jacob emerged from the adjoining room, alertness etched in his posture, as they both stepped back into the evening.

Earlier that afternoon, they had made a discreet stop—guided by Hem—to a local boutique known for low-profile rentals. The invitation made it clear: black tie only. Nothing Cedrela-issued would pass unnoticed.

Hannah chose a floor-length graphite grey gown, sleek and understated, the fabric falling in clean lines that moved like liquid shadow. The neckline sat just off her collarbone, subtle pleats running down one side. A single teardrop earring glinted at her neck, and her dark curls were swept into a loose knot—casual enough to blend, elegant enough not to draw attention.

Jacob wore a charcoal tuxedo tailored just tight enough to hint at Cedrela discipline. The lapel was trimmed in matte satin, and his shirt—crisp and open at the collar—defied a traditional bow tie. His cufflinks bore no insignia, but Hem had embedded a discreet pulse tracker in one. They passed as any European couple attending a diplomatic gala—neutral, polished, forgettable.

Evening deepened around them as they approached the Neo-Gothic theatre Hem had pinpointed. The imposing structure emerged abruptly from shadow, its spires piercing the twilight sky. Once a grand Soviet performance hall for propaganda plays, it now stood quietly forgotten—a perfect space for secrets.

A side door opened silently, revealing a frail, cloaked figure holding a paper lantern. She bowed without a word, stepping back into the shadows.

Inside, Hannah felt her breath catch. Heavy velvet curtains, faded by time, draped elegantly from high, pointed arches. Murals, once proud, depicted Soviet strength and Georgian folklore, now concealed by shadows. The atmosphere pressed down like whispered prayers, sacred and profane at once.

They followed the woman deeper, guided only by the faint glow of lantern light and flickering candles. Down a narrow staircase, the air turned cool, tasting faintly of cedar, wax, and incense.

The subterranean theatre opened up before them, silent and reverent. Antique chairs circled a small stage, each seat occupied by masked figures observing quietly, faces half-hidden by delicate veils. In the center rested an Ottoman-era violin, polished and still—untouched but radiating quiet power.

Four musicians emerged gracefully from shadow, lifting instruments wordlessly. Music filled the vault—delicate, unresolved, powerful. Hannah's heartbeat quickened as the violin at the center vibrated softly, responding as if in silent duet.

Nex spoke calmly in Jacob's ear.

> "Cedrela sequence confirmed active. The violin is responding to external musical stimulus."

Jacob turned slightly, noticing Hannah's tense posture. "You feel it?"

She nodded slightly, unable to speak. Across the circle stood a figure—still, dark-suited, a tulip-shaped pin at his lapel.

"Mehmet's proxy," Hannah breathed.

Jacob's expression tightened. "We're not the only ones who came here prepared."

The music ebbed, leaving an unsettling silence in its wake. Hannah remembered Ethan's words clearly—"Cedrela isn't composed. It's remembered."

She felt something shift in the room around them—a ripple of expectation or dread. They hadn't walked into a gathering.

They had trespassed into the heart of a mystery meant to be protected—or destroyed.

There would be no simple escape from either choice.

The music faded, leaving the chamber suspended in reverent silence.

No applause. No nods of approval. Only stillness—and the sound of breath. Controlled, disciplined, as though every guest had been trained not just to observe, but to obey.

It hadn't been a performance. It had been an invocation.

The violin rested motionless at the centre of the stage, its polished surface glowing in the low, flickering light. It didn't need to be touched to speak.

Jacob leaned subtly toward Hannah, murmuring under his breath, "Hem says Cedrela resonance is stable. Nex confirms Ottoman encryption—variant three. The wood dates back to the 1800s. Probably royal court issue."

Hannah's eyes flicked back to the violin, her voice barely above a whisper. "Tanzimat era?"

He nodded. "Nex thinks so."

Tanzimat.

The word curled in her mind like smoke. It meant reorganisation—a series of sweeping reforms during the 19th century that had tried to modernise the Ottoman Empire from the inside out. Laws were rewritten, schools secularised, bureaucracies expanded. But artists, scholars, and musicians—those who resisted standardisation—had often disappeared.

"Tanzimat was the illusion of enlightenment," she whispered. "But the price was silence. Especially for those who composed truth."

Jacob's brow furrowed slightly, understanding settling behind his eyes.

A tall figure stepped slowly onto the stage, draped in ceremonial robes the colour of dried oxblood. A translucent half-mask obscured his face, and his movements were careful, choreographed.

The garment was not random. It echoed the traditional Bektashi dervish attire, adapted with theatrical precision—the colour symbolising sacrifice, the cut designed to conceal the person within it. In his left hand, he carried a silver tuning fork. In his right, a velvet-wrapped ledger embossed with Ottoman and Georgian script.

"He's the ceremonial master," Jacob whispered. "Not an auctioneer—a guide."

Nex confirmed quietly in his ear:

> "Role aligns with archival gatekeeper. Not transactional. Symbolic guardian of provenance."

The master bowed to the audience—slow, deliberate, almost mournful—then crossed to the violin. He placed the tuning fork beside it and opened the ledger. His gloved hand hovered over a list—symbols, numbers, names—and stopped without touching the page.

The violin.

Another bow. A hush moved through the seated guests like a ripple through smoke.

And then he stepped back into the shadows.

Nex's voice whispered in Jacob's ear.

> "Signal degradation noted. Emotional resonance weakening. Cedrela spiral incomplete."

Jacob leaned in again. "They're waiting for someone to awaken it."

Hannah's gaze drifted across the circle—and found him.

The man with the tulip pin. He was standing now. Maskless. His face was forgettable—deliberately so. But there was a gravity to him, the kind of presence trained to linger in memory only when it was too late.

"He's Mehmet's proxy," she whispered.

Jacob's jaw flexed. "Then this just turned tactical."

Around them, subtle shifts began. A guest adjusted their chair. Another glanced toward a velvet-draped corridor. Silence thickened. Expectation crackled.

"Phantom spike, Hem," Jacob murmured.

A pulse flickered through the theatre. One of the overhead sconces flared, fizzled. Another flickered out completely.

A few masked guests stirred. One half-rose. A whisper passed in Georgian.

Jacob took Hannah's wrist. "Now."

They moved smoothly, as if rehearsed—shoulders low, steps angled sideways toward the periphery. They slipped between the last row of chairs and the velvet drapes just as a string of notes, residual from the tuning fork, hummed faintly through the air.

Behind them, a voice slipped through the dark:

"Truth isn't remembered. It's rerouted."

Hannah turned sharply. The voice was male. Soft. Familiar.

But no one stood there.

"Han—move."

They ducked through the curtain, down a tight corridor lit only by emergency bulbs that glowed like dying embers.

A flight of stairs spiraled downward—bare stone, damp edges, candle smoke still clinging to the walls.

Hem spoke through Jacob's ear:

"Multiple heat signatures approaching. Estimated intercept in thirty seconds. Basement-level exit confirmed. East side. Concealed panel."

"Two pursuers," Jacob muttered, loud enough for Hannah to hear. "Mehmet's network."

She nodded once, tightening her grip on the violin now wrapped inside Jacob's coat. "They don't want it back. They want what it unlocks."

At the corridor's end, a rusted steel door. Jacob shoved it open. They spilled into night.

The cold hit first—then the silence. Behind them, the theatre rose like a tomb. Still. Watching.

A shadow moved in the doorway.

Jacob turned. The man charged.

No mask. No words.

Just movement.

They collided near the alley wall. Jacob blocked the first blow, redirected the second. The man was fast, trained. But not faster.

Jacob slammed him backward. The tulip pin flew off his chest, landing near the gutter.

A breath passed between them—like recognition unspoken.

Then the man turned and fled into the darkness.

Jacob stooped, picked up the pin. Heavy. Sharpened along the edge. Real.

Nex spoke, his voice registering faint alarm:

> "Encryption confirmed. Mehmet's glyph. Early pre-Lale
> signature. Archive embedded."

Behind him, Hannah stared down at the violin, her face pale in the moonlight. Her voice was quiet. Uncertain.

"This wasn't an archive," she said. "It was an offering."

She looked up slowly, eyes catching Jacob's.

"And he knew someone would bleed for it."

They ran.

Not in panic—but with intention, sliding through shadows like ink through script. The Abanotubani district—the oldest in Tbilisi—twisted around them, its stone alleys alive with centuries of ghosts.

Here, in the cradle of steam and sulphur, history clung to every tile and brick. Georgian kings, Persian envoys, Ottoman governors—all had walked these same paths. Some seeking rest. Others seeking silence.

Jacob led, fast but calculating. Hannah followed close, her breath measured, the violin pressed tight to her ribs beneath her coat like a living relic.

Nex pulsed softly in Jacob's ear:

"Surveillance net disrupted. Thermal trail dispersing.
One pursuit vector remains—estimated two agents.
West alley flank."

"Hem says left," Jacob muttered, angling them past a shuttered bazaar. "Toward the old sulphur domes."

They entered a wide square framed by rounded bathhouse roofs, tiled in salmon-pink and charcoal. The smell hit instantly—pungent sulphur, damp clay, and time-warmed stone. The domes steamed faintly, breathing.

"These baths..." Hannah whispered. "They've been operating for over a thousand years."

Jacob nodded. "Ottoman-era governors held secret summits here. Bektashi dervishes met in the lower vaults."

In Ottoman times, bathhouses weren't just for washing—they were sanctuaries, power hubs, confessionals. Secrets were traded in steam. Lives negotiated between cold tiles and burning water.

Even now, locals came to the Abanotubani baths not only for healing—but for connection. Deals struck. Memories buried.

That made it perfect for Mehmet's network.

"Communal trust, layered history, no surveillance," Jacob whispered. "It's the kind of place he'd anchor a proxy cell."

Hannah glanced toward one bathhouse entrance, its mosaic arch slightly cracked. "It's sacred. But it's also vulnerable."

The contrast hit hard. What once healed the body was now used to manipulate the truth.

Hem pinged again.

"Exit corridor narrowed. Courtyard breach ahead. Right turn required. Agents closing at nine metres."

They slipped under an arched breezeway, across a bridge where vines curled like script. The statue of King Vakhtang I Gorgasali loomed above—his outstretched hand shadowing the alley. Legend claimed he had founded Tbilisi where his falcon fell—onto a hot spring.

Jacob remembered the myth, barely catching his breath. "City born where something wild collapsed into fire."

Hannah muttered, "Like Cedrela."

They passed beneath his shadow and entered a collapsed courtyard—mosaics fractured under their feet, vines split by centuries of frost. A mural of Queen Tamar, Georgia's warrior monarch, peeked through ivy.

Jacob pushed open a rusted gate. They emerged again onto a narrow road, climbing toward the Metekhi rise.

The church stood above them now, stone-gray and silent, floodlit against the dark. The air sharpened, carrying the scent of riverwater and ozone.

They reached the plaza below—breathless, hearts hammering.

Jacob crouched by a stone trough, pulse in his ears.

Hannah leaned into the wall, knuckles white around the violin case. She stared up at Metekhi Church, her voice flat and raw.

"Do you know what this place was?"

Jacob shook his head.

"An execution site. Back in the 13th century. And later, during Ottoman control, it became a barracks. Then a prison. Now it's a sanctuary again." She exhaled shakily. "The city forgets. But the stones don't."

Nex pinged gently.

"Pursuit dropped. Agent signature lost. Tactical retreat confirmed."

Jacob let his body sag against the stone, only slightly.

They sat in silence for a moment, surrounded by the hum of ancient geography and political myth.

Hannah looked at the violin resting in her lap. Her voice dropped.

"I used to believe Ethan brought Cedrela to life."

Jacob glanced at her.

"But now... I think Cedrela was always alive. It was just waiting for the right instrument."

He looked away. "Do you think we were supposed to find it?"

"No." Her answer was immediate. "I think we were supposed to protect it. From them. From ourselves."

Jacob's hand drifted to his coat pocket, where the tulip pin lay cold and sharp. "This whole trail—it's not a map. It's a warning."

Hannah's gaze locked onto his.

"What if Ethan didn't just fear what Cedrela could become?" she whispered. "What if he feared what we'd become, if we used it wrong?"

A silence settled between them.

Not final.

But full.

A bell rang once, high above, from the church tower.

Not for prayer.

For memory.

They were no longer running.

They were stepping deeper into legacy.

And the violin?

It vibrated faintly in Hannah's hands.

Not from impact.

But from recognition.

—"This wasn't an archive," she said again, softer now. "It was an offering. And he knew someone would bleed for it."

Chapter Sixteen - Split Threads - Yerevan

The hallway of Tiflis Palace, dimly lit and steeped in age, smelled of old wood, rain, and silence.

They stepped out just after five. Dawn pressed lightly against the windowpanes, casting long grey smears across the marble floor. That strange in-between light where nothing felt certain—not yet day, no longer night.Beneath the hotel's faded awning, the river whispered past unseen, and the cobbled streets were nearly silent—except for the hum of Hem processing too many possibilities.

Their room—third floor, west wing—was now behind a locked door, but it still felt like it watched them leave.

Jacob closed the laptop with a quiet snap. "They'll expect us to move together. We never do. Not in real life, not in chess.'"

Hannah took a breath, stood by the window, arms crossed, her jaw tight.

Jacob continued, "Exactly why we split now."

Hem's voice broke the quiet.

> "Signal spoofing protocol active. Pursuit pattern shows high predictability. Recommending decoupled movement. Separate trajectories will disrupt algorithmic targeting."

Jacob turned to Hannah. "You take the violin and head east. Yerevan."

She didn't move.

"You'll have Hem?"

He nodded. "And Nex. Plus I'll ghost-ping through three servers before I even leave the building."

She exhaled, tension unwinding in strands. "You're sure this isn't just running?"

"No," Jacob said. "This is baiting."

She turned toward the window to compose herself.

You used to disappear, too, she thought. *You shut down when it hurt. After Ethan, you just... folded. But not this time. This time, you stayed.*

She turned back, her voice gentler now. "There was a time I thought you'd ghost again."

Jacob didn't blink. "There was a time I thought I might."

A small, sad smile passed between them. Something reclaimed.

She stepped forward and Jacob gave Hannah a big brother hug and said, "You'll be ok."

"Be safe," she said.

"Be louder," he replied.

Jacob handed Hannah a matte-black capsule, no larger than a matchbox.

"Mini Hem," he said. "With Nex-lite. Local node only. No uplink. No live sync to my feed, but it'll keep eyes on you."

Hannah arched a brow. "Nex-lite?"

Jacob gave her a lopsided smile. "Think of it as Cedrela instincts with none of the sarcasm. You'll get Hem's sweep capability. And Nex's Cedrela reads. They'll talk to each other, not back to me."

She turned the capsule in her hand. "You're sure it's safe to run solo?"

Jacob nodded.

Hannah moved to the table and packed the violin gently in its case—adding two layers of cloth, as if muffling something that still breathed.

She zipped it slowly. "Yerevan, then."

Hem buzzed.

"Train departure confirmed. Platform 3, Tbilisi Central. Identity package accepted. Border protocols seeded. Visa sync preloaded."

"Arzu Kaya," Jacob said, handing over the documents.

"Arzu Kaya?" Hannah raised an eyebrow

Jacob smirked. "Used it once for a contact in Naples. Got past a biometric gate and into an Italian wedding invitation list in the same day. Nearly got us arrested, but the cake was excellent."

"It's clean," Jacob added. "Hem scrubbed the metadata and cross-fed new travel history. She's never left Turkey. Not officially."

A faint smile passed between them. But it faded as she glanced at the street.

"So you stay here. Run interference."

She stared at him for a moment—eyes tired, but steady. "You still think we're ahead?"

"I think we're exactly where Ethan wanted us to be."

Silence bloomed between them. The kind that felt like both a wound and a trust fall.

She stepped forward. Their foreheads touched for half a second—brief, grounding.

"Don't get clever," she whispered. "Just don't get caught."

Jacob smirked. "I'm always clever. That's why I get caught."

A pause. Then laughter—quiet and sad and earned.

She opened the door. The hallway yawned before her like a corridor through fog.

Jacob watched her leave without looking back.

Tbilisi Central Station stood like a contradiction—glass and concrete laid over the bones of a late-Soviet-era structure, flanked by digital billboards and flaking murals. Once, this hub had connected Russian empire lines to Ottoman caravan routes. Now it ferried tourists, traffickers, and tired workers back and forth across invisible lines.

The departure board flickered as Hannah passed through the entry gate.

Nex-lite pinged quietly in her ear:

"Border scan clear. Identity match confirmed. Cabin assignment: First Class – Car 4, berth 1."

She blinked. First class?

The kiosk clerk handed her the ticket with a nod, not even raising an eyebrow.

As Hannah stepped onto the platform, the train awaited like a polished memory—gleaming silver exterior with wine-red trim.Its sides etched with the Georgian rail crest and a row of curtained windows that shimmered in the mist.

The Tbilisi–Yerevan train line had once been the pride of Soviet tourism. Diplomats, smugglers, and musicians had all ridden it. The tracks wove through ravines, rose over ancient river bridges, and bent past border towns like old gods exhaling smoke.

Inside, the first-class cabin surprised her.

Her cabin smelled of cedar and polish. Plush velvet seats. Brass reading lamps. A tiny table folded against the wall beside a window wide enough to frame whole hillsides. A polished wooden ledge held a glass water carafe and a linen napkin. The light switch clicked like an antique.

She exhaled slowly, lowering herself into the seat. The violin case rested across her lap like something asleep.

Nex-lite chimed.

"Visa auto-confirmation successful. Arrival support in Yerevan terminal confirmed. Secure corridor mapped."

"Thanks," she whispered, touching the device like it was alive.

The train shuddered once, then pulled into motion.

Outside, Tbilisi blurred—old roofs, tram cables, onion domes fading into the grey. Then hills. Then quiet.

She pulled out her tablet and opened the Cedrela archive. Files Ethan had flagged. Journal clippings. A musicologist's unfinished study on tonal frequencies. A forgotten conference paper titled "Emotion as Memory Syntax: Cedrela and the Sonic Substrate."

She scrolled. Scanned. Stared.

Nothing leapt out. But she didn't expect it to.

Sometimes Ethan's genius wasn't in what he said—but what he skipped.

She sat back, closed her eyes.

FLASHBACK

It was during their first year of graduate studies.

They'd both been invited to a cross-discipline symposium in Lyon. The university had put them in the same AirBnB by mistake.

She'd arrived first. Tired, late, annoyed.

He walked in carrying three baguettes, four types of cheese, and a notebook.

"I come bearing peace," he'd said. "And lactose."

They'd spent that night cross-legged on the kitchen floor, comparing theses and notes and biases. He asked her what she thought Cedrela felt like.

She'd said, "a tuning fork dipped in regret."

He'd smiled. "I think it's the opposite. I think Cedrela is the sound of regret refusing to stay quiet."

Back then, he'd had a way of seeing sound that made her forget what silence meant.

The train crossed a bridge that curved over nothing but fog. The river below was invisible, but its presence was loud.

She pressed her head to the window.

The violin sat in its case. Silent. But somehow... not.

And in the space between dusk and arrival, Hannah didn't feel like prey anymore.

She felt like the one who remembered.

But not by Mehmet.

By a memory.

And maybe... by someone who still hoped she'd get this right.

The train had been moving for four hours now. Just over 3 more hours to go.

Hannah sat curled against the cabin wall, tablet in one hand, the violin in its case beside her like a sleeping dog.

The carriage swayed gently as the line curved through the southern ridges of Georgia—past dusty vineyards, abandoned rail switches, and river valleys etched like forgotten staves in a score.

She hadn't eaten. The memory of Ethan's notes had chased her appetite away.

Nex-lite pinged softly in her ear.

"Anomaly in file structure. Archive: Goldstein_112. Sequence titled Not for performance. Encrypted attachment—audio-visual hybrid. Partial decryption available."

"Play it," she whispered.

A faint hum rose—off-pitch at first, like tuning gone wrong. Then—overlaying it—Ethan's voice, blurred and stammered, layered beneath footage of something...

She froze. It was an aerial scan. Coordinates she didn't recognise. Trees. A hollowed-out structure. The file cut off mid-frame, glitching at the final timestamp.

Nex-lite added:

"Geotag corresponds to vicinity outside Kars, Eastern Turkey. Logged 7 months before Ethan's disappearance. Discrepancy in date suggests backdated file masking."

Her fingers tightened.

Hem-lite buzzed immediately after:

"Potential sensor breach. Cabin door proximity tripped 3.2 seconds ago. No visual on corridor. Motion trail inconsistent with staff pattern."

Hannah didn't move. Her eyes scanned the door. Nothing. No sound. No shadow under the frame.

But something else moved—inside her.

An anomaly. A file Ethan had hidden from everyone. Buried inside his Cedrela archive. Labeled as something never meant to be performed. Disguised. Dated to throw off anyone tracking his movements. And now it pointed toward Kars—a place no one had mentioned in years.

And Nex-lite—Jacob's distilled AI copy—had pulled it out from the silence like a whisper shaped by guilt.

This was how Ethan thought. Not in answers, but in echoes. He didn't leave trails. He left distortions. Loops. Glitches you had to feel, not find.

And now Hem was warning her someone else might've felt it too.

Still—she palmed the capsule in her pocket, pressing the silent trigger for passive trace sync. Nex-lite would record everything from now until disembarkation.

She exhaled slowly, never taking her eyes off the corridor.

Let the train keep moving.

Let the ghost wait its turn.

She didn't sleep after that.

The train crawled into Yerevan Railway Station just after 2:30 p.m.

Hannah stepped off the platform, blinking against the copper-white glare. The air here felt different—hotter, drier. And heavier, somehow. Like it remembered too much.

The station itself—built in 1956 atop earlier Ottoman transport routes—was a vast semi-circle of marble and red stone, its arches drawing the eye upward toward a spire shaped like a

Soviet-era bayonet. It had been a hub for Silk Road goods, Armenian soldiers, smugglers, and now commuters on borrowed time.

Nex-lite pinged again.

> "Yerevan Terminal mesh is shallow. Passive surveillance only. Interference clean. Temperature spike registered three minutes ago—potential tail."

Then, more gently:

> "Safe route to hotel pre-seeded. Vehicle approaching in 3 minutes."

Outside, the city buzzed low—trolleybuses hissed past faded cafes, street hawkers sold watermelon in slices as wide as books, and an accordionist played "Kele-Kele" beneath the brass Lenin statue that now pointed toward a pedestrian mall.

In the distance, Mount Ararat rose like a secret remembered too late.

The mountain wasn't just beautiful—it was mythic.

Said to be the final resting place of Noah's Ark. Revered in Armenian poetry. Feared in Ottoman campaigns. Claimed and exiled by borders that shifted too often to hold faith.

It was beautiful, yes.

But also scarred.

Just like Cedrela.

Her taxi driver dropped her outside Hotel National—a sandstone-fronted historic hotel just off Republic Square, once a residence for Soviet elite, now restored with velvet lounges, hidden gardens, and a hush that felt like diplomacy.

Hem-lite buzzed as she entered the atrium.

"Biometric sweep clear. No shadow nodes detected. Facial pattern spread accepted. Room 302 assigned under alias. Window faces eastern quarter. Two exits. Elevator monitored."

Just nodded at the concierge, and walked straight up to the self-check in counter. Typed in her details as provided by Hem-lite on the check in screen and waited for her door card to be dispatched from the device next to the screen. Grabbed her card and rode the elevator in silence.

Room 302 held the same kind of stillness Ethan used to crave—quiet, ornate, untouched. Walnut desk. Wide window. She opened it and leaned out slightly.

Below, the city hummed. Beyond it, Ararat waited.

She turned and opened the violin case.

Still there. Still warm.

But when she lifted the instrument, she noticed something new—an edge along the sound post, like a scratch.

She ran her fingertip over it. Not a flaw.

A word.

Etched in Ottoman script.

Nex-lite pulsed softly:

"Engraving detected. Translates to: *The silence that listens.*"

Hannah exhaled.

Not just a message.

A promise.

Nex-lite pinged.

"Target contact: Dr. Arman Tevanyan. Ethnomusicologist. Former advisor to Goldstein. Fired from Vanadzor Conservatory after presenting Cedrela frequency experiments without state clearance."

Hannah murmured, "Where is he now?"

"Works from home. Outskirts of Kond district. Archival flat above a shuttered music school."

She took another sip of the herbal tea she just brewed and placed the cup on the desk and stood-up.

Kond was the oldest inhabited district in Yerevan, and one of its most neglected. It had survived empires, earthquakes, and redevelopment attempts. Once an Ottoman quarter. Then a Soviet slum. Now—unclaimed, unregulated, unrepentant.

Shops operated from inside garages. Grandmothers sat outside metal doors, cracking sunflower seeds beside revolutionary graffiti. Children kicked footballs against walls with Persian tiles buried under concrete. Condemned buildings clung to the hills like tired sentries. Windows stared back without glass.

But under it all—still beating—was resistance.

Kond wasn't a place people visited. It was a place they remembered wrong.

And that, Hannah thought, is why Ethan sent her here.

Hannah found the address easily. A rusted gate. A stairwell. An unmarked door.

She knocked once.

A voice called out, "I'm not taking commissions!"

"I'm not selling," she replied.

Silence.

Then the bolt slid.

The man who opened the door looked like he'd argued with gravity his whole life and lost gracefully. His beard was grey, his eyes sharp. He wore a paint-stained cardigan over a faded conservatory shirt.

"Goldstein?" he asked.

"Mrs Goldstein" she said.

His mouth twitched. "Then you should come in very quietly."

The flat was a mausoleum of music.

Reels of cassette tape coiled across shelves. Handwritten scores stacked waist-high. A dulcimer leaned against a radiator. The walls bore black-and-white photos of protest choirs, microphones wrapped in barbed wire.

"Ethan left something behind," she said, once seated.

"He left many things behind," Dr. Arman replied, placing two cups of black tea on the table. "Some of them were not welcome."

She nodded, gently lifting the violin case and setting it between them.

He didn't touch it. He just looked at her.

"He was working on Cedrela as if it were alive," he said. "Because to him, it was. Not just code. Not even music. But a structure that learned from the person playing it."

She opened the case.

He inhaled sharply. "That belonged to Mahir Çelebi. "Ottoman court musician. Disappeared in 1856. Rumour says he encoded secrets into his performance style. They called him the dissonant whisper."

Dr. Arman's voice dropped lower, as if recalling something no one had written down.

"They say his final performance was at the Dolmabahçe Palace. A private concert—March 1856. Just after the Treaty of Paris. Only the Grand Vizier and the Sultan were present. The score was never archived. No one remembered the melody. But the next morning, Mahir Çelebi was gone. No death record. No exile. Just a note from the palace scribe: *'Performance concluded without replication.'*"

Hannah blinked. "Without replication?"

Dr. Arman nodded. "Couldn't be repeated. Not because it was flawed. Because it was too honest."

"It carries Cedrela," she whispered. "Ethan found it. Or maybe it found him."

Dr. Arman's fingers hovered over the scroll. "This violin was made not just to sound. But to remember."

Nex-lite buzzed gently in Hannah's ear.

"Emotive harmonic pattern detected. Violin material retains resonant imprint. Memory encoded not in notes—but in dissonance."

Dr. Arman sat back. "He always said Cedrela didn't reward the skilled. It revealed the haunted."

Back in Tbilisi, the room was dim but alert.

Jacob sat cross-legged on the rug of their temporary base—an apartment leased for anonymity via Air-bnb, routed through four proxy layers. It wasn't meant for comfort, only for quiet. The walls were thick, old, lined with mismatched books and postcards from strangers who'd never left names. A kettle hummed low on the stove. The scent of over-boiled cardamom clung to the air.

Hem pulsed softly.

"Archive correlation complete. Five distinct Cedrela logic branches identified in metadata clusters traced to Project Lale."

Jacob leaned forward. "How many systems?"

"At least eleven. Six now defunct. Five—public facing."

Nex overlaid the list in Jacob's glasses.

Three media aggregation engines. Two open-source wellness platforms. A language-learning app in beta.

And a meditation app with over 14 million users.

Jacob's pulse quickened.

He brought up the Cedrela variant they'd recovered from the Süleymaniye archive, layered it over the wellness app's back-end audio architecture.

The match wasn't exact.

It was worse.

Hem's voice turned analytical.

"Not duplication. Mimicry. Someone repurposed Cedrela's emotional cueing system into adaptive suggestion logic. Triggered by mood-tagged user inputs. Self-reinforcing. Self-modifying."

Nex clarified for both Jacob and, by extension, us.

"Imagine Cedrela was a song designed to open something inside you—grief, memory, recognition. Someone took that and rewired it into the kind of music that trains algorithms how to read people's feelings in real-time. It doesn't teach. It adapts. It learns what hurts—and echoes it."

Jacob muttered under his breath, "They didn't preserve it... they fed it to the feed."

He scrubbed deeper, tracing the original Project Lale node that first seeded this thread—buried beneath four layers of university grants and a shell think tank out of Ankara. It hadn't been officially funded since 2019.

And yet.

Nex displayed a recent log-in, timestamped two weeks ago. The server tag: Kırmızı_Tulip-Δ63.

Jacob tapped the embedded data string and decrypted a single locked voice note.

It was degraded—audio warped, syllables bent, like listening through fog.

But it was Ethan's voice.

Whispering.

"If they extract it from the structure, they'll never understand the cost. They'll echo the ghost, not the grief. Cedrela... isn't silence. It's what silence guards."

The voice stuttered. Paused.
Then:

"Hannah..."

And the file collapsed into static.

Jacob sat still for a long moment, shoulders tight, his chest hollowed by something that wasn't quite shock. He'd heard Ethan's voice plenty in recordings—lectures, debates, one old voicemail—but this one felt different. It wasn't for anyone else. It was meant to be found by someone who knew what it meant to carry a legacy that might become a weapon.

What Hem and Nex had just uncovered wasn't theory anymore. Cedrela was no longer confined to dusty manuscripts or coded melodies hidden in violins. It was now humming beneath digital surfaces—coiled into scroll bars, embedded in background tones, influencing how people clicked, paused, even breathed while listening.

It was replicating. Quietly. Unseen.

A contagion disguised as insight.

Hem spoke again.

> "One of the apps just ran a silent update. Deployment set for midnight UTC. Emotional-response loop activated. Cadence consistent with Cedrela spike behaviour."

Nex followed.

> "It's already inside the feedback systems. Hannah was right. It's no longer contained."

Jacob stood slowly. His hands moved automatically—scrubbing the trace, sealing the encrypted logs, and initiating a ghost key wipe of the decrypted file.

He sent a message—through their private secured channel, one of Ethan's original relay codes reactivated only once since Istanbul. The kind of line that never left residue.

In Yerevan, Hannah sat on the rooftop of the Hotel National.

The violin case rested beside her, unopened. The city glowed in copper tones below—cathedral domes, Stalinist ruins, rooftop gardens humming with music and smoke.

Mount Ararat loomed in the distance, black against the fading purple sky.

She was supposed to depart Yerevan to Kars in the morning—but Dr. Arman had offered to show her one more lead. A conservatory with Ethan's name on the guest registry. She had agreed, without hesitation.

They met just before sunset, outside the crumbling Komitas Chamber Conservatory, a narrow stone building tucked behind a bus depot in central Yerevan. Arman introduced her to Anahit Davtyan, a retired violinist and former ethnomusicologist who once lectured on forgotten Ottoman instruments. Her wrists trembled slightly when she spoke, but her memory was crystalline.

> "He came once," Anahit had said, guiding Hannah through a narrow corridor that smelled of varnish and dust. "Didn't speak much. Listened more than he played."

Anahit handed Hannah a photocopy from the conservatory's archive—a guestbook entry from seven years ago, signed in Ethan's looping script. Below it, in pencil and a different hand, was a scrawled note:

"Trebizond, not Venice. Ask the one who still listens."

She also gave Hannah a small, tarnished brass tuning fork in a velvet pouch.

"He left this with me. Said the right frequency would reveal the rest."

Hannah had held it for a long moment before slipping it into the inside pocket of her coat. She didn't ask what Anahit meant by "the rest."

Before she left, Anahit had hesitated.

"There was a man," she said softly. "A former musicologist—once attached to a Cedrela-linked project Ethan quietly funded. He moved east after the funding stopped. Near the old citadel in Kars."

She hadn't offered a name. Only a description.

"He listened differently," Anahit said. "You'll know him by what he doesn't say."

That same hour, Hem relayed something unexpected to Jacob: a low-frequency signal burst had registered on a Cedrela monitoring thread—barely a ghost trace, but consistent with Ethan's archived voice pattern. It had lasted four seconds.

The origin point: just west of Kars fortress perimeter.

They didn't need to speak. She would drive from Yerevan. He would take the line down from Erzurum.

Now back in her hotel, she sat alone. Not afraid. But aware.

She checked her phone.

Her fingers hovered above the reply button.

But there was no reply for something like that.

Only the wind.

And the faint, persistent echo of a melody that didn't want to be forgotten.

One message.

—"You're right. It's not a cipher. It's a contagion. And someone just let it out."

Chapter Seventeen - Buried Notes

The wind in Kars didn't whistle—it mourned. Low, aching currents moved through the stone streets like something left unsaid. Snow had settled overnight, softening the broken lines of a city built from siege and memory.

Hannah crossed the Armenian border at dawn.

The drive had taken just over six hours across cold, vast terrain—first along the white-blanketed highlands outside Yerevan, then southwest past Mount Ararat, its peak invisible in the morning cloud. The final stretch ran through Doğubayazıt, once an Ottoman military stronghold and a Silk Road watchpoint.

In her coat pocket, the velvet pouch pressed lightly against her ribs. Inside it, the tarnished tuning fork Anahit Davtyan had given her. And folded beside it, a photocopied page from a guestbook—Ethan's name inked clean across one line, and beneath it, in a stranger's hand:

"Trebizond, not Venice. Ask the one who still listens."

She hadn't needed a second reading. Whatever Ethan had uncovered in Yerevan, it hadn't ended in sound. It had begun with silence—and someone who still knew how to hear it.

The mountains fell behind her. Kars rose quietly ahead.

Its fortress ruins still clung to the hillside, overlooking the town like a half-closed eye.

Doğubayazıt had history carved into its bones—battles, pacts, betrayals. Centuries ago, it was the staging post for imperial armies pushing east into Persia. Now, it was dusted with snow and suspicion, the kind of town that hadn't forgotten how to watch strangers.

The border guards lingered over her passport. Hannah kept her eyes down.

"ID confirmed. Rental vehicle authorised."

Hem's voice, crisp in her ear.

"Car registered to Leila Yılmaz. Turkish ID code pre-seeded and clean."

Hem had arranged everything. The rental, the fake name, the faded scarf around her neck that matched old security footage from four years ago.

By the time she reached Kars, just pass noon, her coat smelled of road dust and melted snow.

Jacob would arrive two hours later.

She parked in front of the Kars train station, engine off, watching the incoming route from Erzurum. The old Soviet-style building across the road had its shutters drawn. Snow gathered quietly on the platform edge.

She found a quiet café with fogged-up windows and no music—just the sound of a kettle cycling through its breath. The coffee was dark and bitter, but it burned the cold from her hands. She sat by the window, watching the track bend toward the horizon, where the sky and snow seemed to merge and watching the incoming route from Erzurum. The old Soviet-style building across the road had its shutters drawn. She lingered over the coffee, breaking open a Kars kaşar börek—the outer pastry crisp, the cheese inside sharp and salty, aged in the cold air of mountain caves. The warmth spread through her chest as she ate slowly, letting the steam rise and mingle with the breath on the windowpane.

The hiss of steam triggered a memory she hadn't summoned in years.

FLASHBACK

A different café. Different cold. Vienna, the winter she and Ethan had nearly missed the conference keynote because he insisted on finding the "original" Sachertorte—not the tourist kind, but the one an old woman made in a tiled basement across the canal. He had called it "memory by taste." She had called it ridiculous.

And then, he'd looked at her and said, "We never remember the safe days, Hannah. Only the strange ones."

She hadn't said it aloud then, but she remembered thinking: You remember everything, Ethan. Even the things I try to forget.

Hem-lite whispered in her ear.

"Incoming," "Private freight segment diverted. One passenger disembarking. ID match confirmed."

When she stood to leave, she slid a few crisp lira notes onto the saucer and turned to the shopkeeper. "Two more, please," she said, gesturing to the börek. The woman smiled knowingly and wrapped them carefully in wax paper. "For someone waiting?" she asked in Turkish. Hannah nodded. "Someone always is."

Outside, the wind whipped sideways. She stepped out with the parcel under her arm and crossed toward the station. Her boots made hollow prints in the snow.

Hem pinged gently.

"Platform access optimal via southern staircase. Jacob arrival confirmed. Estimated visual in one minute."

She adjusted her scarf and quickened her pace. The station loomed ahead—etched in frost, holding its breath.

Jacob stepped off the steel step of a cargo carriage that hadn't carried passengers in decades. His coat was darker than usual, collar upturned against the wind. He carried no bag—only what he could wear and remember.

His route had begun in Tbilisi, but the critical stretch was the one through Erzurum, a city once called the citadel of the Ottomans. It had been the imperial buffer zone—religious, military, defiant. Now its rail yards serviced more memories than maps.

Hem had rerouted a Cedrela-linked supply run from Erzurum to Kars—an old freight line still maintained for logistical training. Jacob travelled in the only car not listed in public schedules.

He reached her, then she stepped in and wrapped her arms around him—tight, brief, but real.

"You're late," she murmured against his coat.

"You're early," he replied, pulling back with a wry grin.

She handed him the parcel. "Local favourite. Kars kaşar börek. Eat it before it freezes."

Jacob opened it, the steam rising. "You always bribe me with carbs when you're worried."

"And you always eat them, even when you're not."

They began walking across the platform toward the street, boots crunching softly in rhythm. Behind them, the train hissed like a sigh.

"Didn't think I'd miss the smell of Turkish trains," Jacob said, glancing sideways.

Hannah shrugged. "Memory by taste. Or something like that."

"Strange days," he said, and this time, it wasn't a joke.

Kars Castle rose above the city—its black stone frame dusted in white, perched like a sentinel on the ridge. Built in 1153 and restored by the Ottomans, it had once guarded the empire's edge against Russian incursions. Now it overlooked schoolyards and satellite dishes, as though memory still required protection.

The provincial archive sat in its shadow, inside a former seminary. A long stone building with weatherworn doors and the smell of coal smoke in its lintels. It wasn't warm, but it was alive.

Emine Karaca stood just inside the arched stone entrance to the old seminary, where snow collected in quiet drifts along the courtyard steps. A weather-worn inscription above the gate marked it as once holy ground—now a vault of memory. Her wool shawl hugged close to her frame, and her gaze studied them both with the patience of someone used to silence.

Emine didn't speak at first—just turned and led them through the arched stone entryway. The courtyard unfolded like a forgotten stanza: colonnades draped in icicles, cracked mosaic tiles beneath the snow, and the faint scent of wood smoke drifting from an unseen brazier. Stone benches lined the walls, worn smooth by generations of scholars who once debated under stars now buried by cloud. Above them, the black silhouette of Kars Castle loomed, visible through the open archways—its presence not threatening, but ancestral. Wind brushed through the inner cloister like a hymn missing its last note. Hannah caught the scent of old ink and damp parchment as they stepped inside, her boots echoing faintly against the vaulted corridor. Memory had weight here—not just Ethan's, but something older, bone-deep.

"He didn't tell me his name," she said. "Just that he was preserving something that didn't belong to him."

She handed Jacob a leather folder. The stitching was old. The paper inside—older still.

Most of the pages bore Ottoman-era notation: dervish invocations, imperial marches, funeral hymns.

But one sheet was different.

Lighter. The ink shimmered faintly. A single tulip was drawn in the corner. Ethan's tulip.

Next to it: a message in clean, deliberate handwriting.

"Memory embedded. Playback requires silence and resonance. If you're hearing this, it's because I doubted—and still trusted."

Hannah held the page like glass. "It's him."

Jacob nodded and activated Hem. Nex flickered to life.

"Acoustic filament detected. Ethan Goldstein voiceprint matched. Initialising resonance playback."

The room deepened.

Ethan's voice unfurled slowly. No distortion. No filters.

"If you're listening... I didn't make the next handover. Or I did—and it didn't matter anymore. Someone inside Cedrela gave Orion information. Not by mistake. Out of conviction."

He sounded tired. Not weak—but heavy.

"I believed we were incorruptible. That truth protected itself. I was wrong."

"I won't name them. You'll know them by silence. And if you've come this far, you already feel it."

A pause. Then softer:

"This isn't a warning. It's an apology. I tried to keep you safe by hiding meaning inside beauty. But beauty, Hannah, is never neutral. It remembers everything."

Silence.

"Playback complete," Nex confirmed. "No data trace detected."

They didn't speak.

Then Nex pulsed again.

"Incoming message. Encrypted. Source: unknown. Format: video. Decryption complete."

Jacob's glasses lenses brightened.

Mehmet.

Not live. A timed recording. Firelight danced on the edge of his silhouette.

"Curiosity, Hannah... is loyalty wearing a different name."

Her heart clenched.

"Ethan thought Cedrela could remain untouched. He thought memory served justice. But memory needs a master."

He leaned into the light.

"This isn't betrayal. This is what comes after. And you've always been part of it."

The video cut.

Nex flickered.

"Self-erasure complete. Embedded trace neutralised."

Jacob stood, already moving. "We need to leave. Now."

Hannah didn't ask where.

Outside, the wind didn't welcome them.

It warned.

They didn't speak again until they were on the road.

Kars fell behind them slowly, its silhouette dissolving into snow and fog. Hannah kept her eyes forward, knuckles tense on the steering wheel. Jacob adjusted Hem's receiver to jam local tracking bands, then double-checked the signal cloak.

"We're clean," he said quietly.

She nodded but didn't reply. Not yet.

The silence between them was old—not heavy, not hostile. Just worn down by years of learning how not to hurt each other.

It was Hannah who finally spoke.

"He knew someone would betray him," she said. "And he still left the page."

Jacob leaned back, watching the frost form delicate patterns on the side mirror. "He needed you to know he doubted. And that he still trusted you."

"That's not fair." Her voice caught. "I'm not sure I would've done the same."

"You would've," Jacob assured her. "You just wouldn't have left it behind."

He didn't look at her as he said it, but the conviction in his voice steadied something in her. A reminder that they still believed in each other—even if belief felt like a brittle thing now.

A half-smile broke on her lips, and it hurt more than it healed.

They turned off the main road, guided by Hem's local overlay, and drove another fifteen minutes in near silence. The snow deepened with altitude, swallowing the landscape in thick folds. Boğatepe appeared like a memory from another century—stone homes half-buried in white, chimney smoke curling into the wind, and silence so complete it felt reverent. Just past the last livestock fence, Hem pulsed.

"Target confirmed. Structure 19.8 meters ahead. Former dairy cooperative. Cache integrity: 94%."

The farmhouse was a skeletal frame of basalt stone, its roof collapsed inward and its wooden beams darkened by age and storms. Locals once made cheese here—famed kaşar and gravyer aged in caves now sealed by frost and disuse. Hannah parked just inside the broken gate. The Cedrela mark—three vertical notches carved beneath a frosted windowsill—was barely visible. A sign only those taught to look would ever find.

"It feels like he left breadcrumbs knowing we'd be desperate enough to follow," she said. Her voice was quiet, but not uncertain.

"We need to talk about what he said," Jacob added.

She raised an eyebrow.

"'Not by accident. Out of belief.'" He quoted Ethan word for word. "That means ideology. Not money. Someone inside Cedrela isn't leaking—they're shifting."

Hannah exhaled slowly. "I've been thinking it for days. Since Bucharest. Since the Lipscani file. But this confirms it."

They pulled up beside a ruined farmhouse—roof collapsed, windows boarded. Inside, the cache room was clean and dry, lined with thermal blankets and water packets. A small burner hummed softly in the corner.

Hannah sat cross-legged on the floor, holding the parchment Ethan had encoded. The tulip shimmered under the LED torchlight.

"Do you think he was... broken, when he recorded that?" she asked.

Jacob hesitated. "No. I think he was clear."

"Clear?"

"Clarity's different from peace. He didn't sound resigned. He sounded like he finally understood the cost."

Hannah was silent for a long beat. Then she whispered, "It hurts that he didn't warn me. But it would've hurt more if he had."

She stared down at the parchment again.

"I wish we'd talked more. About Cedrela. About his reasons." Her voice grew thinner. "We always talked about the theory. The logic. But never the feeling."

"You both did that," Jacob said, softer. "It was how you protected each other."

He pulled a blanket from the cache stack and laid it gently over her shoulders. "You don't have to protect him anymore. We're here. We can face it."

They sat in the quiet a moment longer.

Then Nex blinked.

"Secondary layer of data detected. Ethan's parchment contains non-acoustic cipher: geometric overlays aligned to musical structure."

Jacob leaned in. "Hidden map?"

Nex responded.

"Possibly. Coordinates pending reconstruction. Estimated resolution: 9 minutes."

From outside, the wind rose suddenly and then dropped—as if something had passed overhead. Hannah looked toward the window, but saw only white.

She closed her eyes, letting the cold settle around her like a second skin.

"Promise me something," she said.

"Anything."

"If it's someone we know—someone close—I want to hear it from you. Not from Hem. Not from Nex."

Jacob looked at her. His voice was steady, but his eyes weren't.

"I promise."

The room had gone quiet. Not with peace—but with tension that hadn't decided what shape to take.

Nex's interface blinked green on the portable screen propped against a crate. A single coordinate sequence pulsed at the top.

"Decryption complete," Nex said. "Target location: 39.7809° N, 42.9910° E. Rural site. No Cedrela infrastructure detected. Probable fallback node. Designation: Echo Vault 7."

Jacob frowned. "That's not a Cedrela archive. It's not even a known cache point."

Hannah leaned closer, reading the lines again.

"It's where we stayed once," she said. "Years ago. Between briefings. He said it had 'clean silence.'"

"You mean Ethan brought you there?"

"Just for a night. It wasn't about the operation." Her voice softened. "It was about... resetting."

Jacob glanced at her, uncertain. "He didn't leave the next clue with Cedrela. He left it with *you*."

She didn't respond. She was already moving.

She reached for the kettle and poured the last of the water into a tin cup. Steam rose lazily. She held it close to her face—not for the warmth, but for the memory it summoned.

Her mind flickered back—Vienna again. But not the Sachertorte. This time, the walk after.

The sky had been grey then, too. Ethan had stopped at a market stall, picked up a small bag of roasted chestnuts. Warm in her hand. Too salty.

"It's not about the taste," he'd told her, "it's about remembering what it cost to get here."

In the present, Hannah whispered, "He didn't leave a trail, Jacob. He left a ritual."

Jacob blinked. "A ritual?"

"Repetition. Place. Sensation. He wasn't protecting data. He was preserving memory."

Nex blinked amber.

> "System warning: Cedrela signature at previous archive site shows timestamp discrepancy. Encryption altered. Origin unknown."

Jacob stiffened. "What kind of discrepancy?"

> "Subtle code drift. Could indicate overwritten echo—external interference."

"Orion?" Hannah asked.

"Unconfirmed. But proximity alert: 312 km east. Signal ping matches Mehmet Orman encryption variant 4-C."

Jacob's expression changed.

"That's one of Mehmet's old digital fingerprints," he explained quietly. "Buried into Cedrela systems years ago. If it's active, it means he's either tracing us... or baiting us."

The tension solidified.

Jacob paced once across the room. "We need to run a delay. Change direction. Let Hem scramble the coordinates and scatter our signal."

"No," Hannah said, rising. "If we wait, we lose the echo."

"You're making this emotional."

"I'm making this *real*." She stepped toward him. "You still think we're tracking Ethan. I think Ethan's tracking *us*."

He didn't reply right away.

Then, softly, "You still trust him."

"No," she said. "I trust what he couldn't say."

They stared at each other—something unspoken trading hands between them.

He'd always been the hinge between them. Ethan with his riddles, Hannah with her razor-edge questions. And now he was the one trying to hold both pieces of their story steady.

Then Nex pinged again.

"Encryption drift moving west. Estimate: 22 km in last 14 minutes."

Hannah looked up sharply. "You think he's close?"

Jacob shook his head. "Not him. But something he's guiding. These pings... they travel faster than he does. It's how he tracks us—by waking the ghosts we left behind."

Outside, a sharp crack echoed off the snow-covered wall. Not gunfire. Not wind.

Just loud enough to not belong.

They both froze.

Jacob muttered "Mehmet's watching, or worse—guiding."

Hannah picked up the parchment again—the tulip still shimmered faintly in the low light. She folded it carefully, almost reverently, and tucked it into the lining of her coat.

They moved without a word. Jacob slid the burner into a sack, Nex packed itself down, and Hem reloaded the exit route with six diverging paths.

Hannah took one last glance at the door.

"It's not about what he left behind," she said. "It's about what he couldn't carry with him."

Jacob nodded once, and that was enough.

They were nearly to the door when the light flickered—twice.

Then Nex's voice, suddenly sharp:

"Multiple incoming pings. Ten kilometers. Closing."

No more conversation.

They ran.

—"Then we find him first. Or we go down proving he mattered."

Chapter Eighteen - The Fold's Origin

The wind chased them down the mountainside.

By the time they reached the car, snow had reclaimed their footprints and Max had gone silent—power-saving mode, Jacob said, but even Hem felt heavier. Hannah didn't speak. She simply drove, following the route Hem marked, one waypoint at a time.

They'd left the cache just outside Boğatepe—the highland village southeast of Kars, not its distant coastal namesake. Ethan had once joked that this place was perfect because no one ever remembered which Boğatepe you meant. Now it seemed less like a joke, and more like a design.

The road narrowed, then disappeared. They parked at the foot of the ridge and continued on foot, boots crunching through layers of untouched snow. The terrain steepened into a rough incline cut with natural stone ledges, skeletal trees, and fractured fencing that had long outlived its purpose.

"Vault entry 120 metres ahead," Hem murmured. "Pulse signal consistent. Masking protocol stable."

Jacob exhaled hard. "This is the farthest I've ever followed Ethan's trail."

Hannah said nothing. Her breath was shallow, chest tight. Every step forward felt like walking into a conversation she wasn't ready to finish—but couldn't bear to leave hanging.

As they rounded a bend, the vault revealed itself.

Carved discreetly into the rockface, half-sunken beneath a jagged basalt overhang, was a steel panel smoothed into natural lines. There were no markings. No seams. Just a cold face of metal embedded in ancient stone, as if the mountain had grown around it.

A whisper in her memory returned—Ethan's voice in Milan, laughing in the dim light of a church-turned-safehouse.

"You don't bury secrets. You fold them."

Hannah stepped forward. She reached beneath her coat and unclipped the pendant from its chain—a flattened obsidian disc with a faint etching only visible when held to firelight.

She held it to the steel.

Nothing.

Then, a click—soft, magnetic—and a low hum like wind in a canyon.

> "Biometric resonance match," Max confirmed. "Ethan Goldstein fallback signature authenticated. Echo Vault 7 access granted."

The steel panel slid aside with a hiss of displaced air, revealing a narrow passageway descending at a sharp angle. The interior walls were stone reinforced with aged Kevlar lining, visible in places where moisture had peeled away the upper seal.

The air that hit her face was cold, but preserved—like a breath held too long.

"Stay close," she whispered, and descended first.

The narrow corridor coiled down into the earth like a root seeking warmth. Their boots echoed along the ribbed floor, damp with condensation. At a landing, the tunnel opened into a wider chamber—low ceiling, steel-framed desk, worn plastic chairs. A backup generator sat boxed near the wall, covered with dust, but intact. Emergency light strips edged the base of the room.

And then—there it was.

Etched into the far wall above a dead terminal, half-lit in the gloom, was a single tulip.

Her heart stuttered. It wasn't the carving itself—it was the way it looked like it had always been there. As though this vault had formed around it, not the other way.

She stepped forward slowly. The air shifted as she moved, and her gloves suddenly felt like a barrier.

She pulled them off—fingers stiff from cold—and reached into her coat pocket. Her hand closed around the velvet pouch. The tuning fork Anahit had given her was still there—cold, small, and strangely heavy. She slipped it out, struck it once, gently, against the steel edge of the desk.

A pure, wavering tone floated into the room.

The tulip glimmered faintly—almost imperceptibly—as if the sound had stirred some memory buried in the stone.

Hannah said nothing. She slid the fork back into her coat, and finally reached out. Her bare palm met the wall.

The tulip was warm.

Jacob said nothing. He just stood beside her, his arm brushing her shoulder.

"I've never seen you hesitate with a symbol," he murmured.

"I've never seen a symbol that remembered me."

Max's voice broke the silence.

"Data terminal linked. Ethan Goldstein legacy cache detected. One message available. Playback integrity: 67%."

That pulled both of them out of the moment.

"Why only sixty-seven?" Hannah asked, withdrawing her hand.

"Metadata corrupted. Possibly partial overwrite. Cross-signature conflict."

Jacob moved to the terminal, fingers flying over the keys. "He knew this place wouldn't stay untouched."

"No," Hannah said. "He knew someone would try to rewrite what he left."

The glow came not from the terminal, but from Nex's embedded lens—projecting softly onto the wall like a breath in winter air. The cache's internal relay pulsed to life, drawing from the vault's emergency reserves. Diagnostic lines scrolled across Nex's interface, curved to fit the surface of Jacob's glasses.

"Initializing playback... Ethan Goldstein voiceprint confirmed," Nex said. "Warning: message integrity compromised. Source material incomplete."

Jacob adjusted the projection settings on his lenses, sharpening the resolution.

As Nex began projecting the playback onto the stone wall, Hannah blinked.

"I didn't know he could do that," she said, watching the soft arc of light curve from Jacob's glasses like a whisper across the room.

Jacob gave a small shrug. "He only does it when the signal integrity drops. Field mode, not standard ops."

Hannah's tone was somewhere between impressed and wary. "Of course you gave your AI a second personality."

Jacob smirked. "One of us has to have backup plans."

Nex's projection remained steady, but it was Hem's internal speaker—embedded beneath the collar seam of Jacob's coat—that carried the voice. Low. Clear. Too present.. Low. Clear. Too present.

Then Ethan's voice filled the room.

Hannah stood still, but something inside her flinched. It had been months since she'd heard his voice—*really* heard it, not in recordings or dreams or algorithmic approximations. And now, even this didn't sound like him. The tone was colder. Clipped. Altered, maybe. Or changed by time and fear. She didn't know if she would ever see him again—or if he was even still alive. What scared her most wasn't losing Ethan. It was losing the *shape* of him. The way he used to say her name. The way he looked away when he was hiding something and thought she wouldn't notice. Those things were fading, and no data cache could bring them back.

"If you've come this far... then the version of me you knew is already gone."

Hannah froze.

"Cedrela was never what I thought. What *we* thought. I left behind what I could, but even memory—especially memory—can be filtered. Framed. Turned into leverage."

"What I buried wasn't truth. It was a fold. A fold inside another fold. The first layer was for you. This one... is for the ones who stayed loyal to Cedrela, even when Cedrela stopped being loyal to us."

He paused.

"If you're still listening, then you're choosing to question everything I taught you."

The screen blinked. Static cut briefly through the audio, and for a moment, Ethan's face appeared—half-lit, grainy, flickering.
His eyes weren't afraid. They were... tired.

"I tried to protect you by keeping you aligned to something that looked like certainty. But certainty is dangerous. It blinds. It edits."

The playback stuttered. Nex chimed:

"Data interruption. Reconstructing buffer..."

When his face appeared—grainy, half-lit—her breath hitched like she'd been punched from the inside. It wasn't just the surprise. It was the way his expression hadn't changed. That same tired kindness in the eyes, that subtle tension in the jaw when he was trying to hold something back. The camera had aged him, pixel by pixel, but her memory hadn't. It hurt—*violently*—to see him not as she remembered, but as he might be now. Somewhere. Or nowhere. Her fingers tightened around the pendant under her coat like it might stop her from unraveling

Hannah stepped back, swallowing hard. "That's not the same voice," she whispered. "That's not the Ethan who left the page in Kars."

Jacob was still staring at the screen. "It's him. But not at the same time. It's like... one part of him trusted us. The other—didn't trust anything anymore."

Nex's voice returned.

"Playback integrity restored. Continuing message..."

"If they're listening too—Mehmet, Orion, even Cedrela command—they'll see this message as a liability. A loose end."

"But memory isn't a liability. It's a choice. And sometimes... it's the only rebellion left."

The screen dimmed. The terminal powered down on its own, the last line still echoing in the room.

It's the only rebellion left.

Hannah's eyes welled. She turned away quickly, but Jacob saw. "You alright, Han?"

"No," she said. "Because this wasn't just a message. It was... his confession. And it doesn't match the man I remember."

Jacob stepped closer. "Or maybe it does. Maybe this is what he became when he realised how much was being rewritten—behind his back."

Hannah looked at him. "So which Ethan do we trust?"

Jacob didn't answer immediately. He sat back slightly, eyes still on the wall where Ethan's shadow had been.

"We all have versions of ourselves," he said finally. "The ones we show to strangers. The ones we hide from the people we love. But the versions we *fold* into others—the ones that shape their lives without asking permission... those are the ones that stay. You don't have to trust the Ethan in this message. You trust the one who folded himself into you. And that's not data, Hannah. That's legacy."

He paused—then softer, almost as if to himself:

"The one who gave you the tulip. Not the one who looked away while someone filtered him."

They stood there in silence, facing a message that had spoken in riddles—and ended with a warning.

Nex pinged again.

> "Residual metadata detected. One embedded cipher remains—concealed in final audio waveform. Extraction requires real-time alignment."

Jacob leaned forward slightly, his voice low.

"That means he buried a second layer. Not in the words—but in the sound itself. The pitch, the pauses, maybe even the static. It's not what he said—it's how he said it."

Hannah's jaw tightened. "So we listen again. And this time, we listen differently."

The room was still, but the silence no longer felt neutral.

Nex's voice cut through it like the first crack in ice:

> "Cipher alignment underway. Pattern suggests embedded map data—non-visual. Audio-layered encryption."

Jacob moved to the far desk, pulling out a compact directional mic from his kit. "We'll need to isolate the waveform by tone range. Highs, mids, and hiss-laced decay—he used static like a signature."

Hannah nodded, but her focus was on the wall. The tulip carving glowed faintly again, the emergency light casting it in a new shadow, benting sharper - like a scar instead of a symbol. She reached out and touched it once more—not to decode it, but to steady herself.

"You ever think he meant for us to find this after everything fell apart?" she asked.

Jacob looked over. "He built this place like a lifeboat."

"Yeah," she said softly. "Only lifeboats don't work if you don't know you're drowning."

Her breath caught before Nex even spoke. For a second, she wasn't in the vault—she was in Paris, under rainlight, listening to Ethan hum a song she never asked the name of.

"You remember the notes, not the melody," he'd said once. "That's how memory survives the truth."

He had smiled then. She hadn't realised it was goodbye.

Nex pinged sharply.

"Alignment complete. Cipher resolved. Coordinate string extracted. Overlaying now."

The wall beside the tulip shifted—just pixels on stone, lit up by Nex's projection.

A second location. A final fallback. Farther south. Closer to Cedrela's original field deployment zone.

"Destination registered," Nex said. "Legacy cache Echo-9. Risk grade: high. Asset trace confirms recent digital access—timestamp: thirty-four hours ago."

Jacob straightened. "Someone's already been there."

"Or they're waiting for us to be stupid enough to walk in," Hannah muttered.

Hem pinged for the first time in an hour.

"Alert: low-signal interference pattern detected. Not proximity. Ambient anomaly. Passive drift echo."

Jacob's expression tightened. "That's not static. That's bleed. Someone's running active trace layering."

Hannah turned sharply. "So this was the bait?"

"No," he said. "This was the filter. The bait's already working."

She looked at him—eyes sharp now. "How bad?"

Nex responded first.

"If their signal's bouncing off our trace, we've got twelve minutes max before overlap."

Hannah's hand found the parchment again, almost instinctively. "He knew. Even this deep in, he knew."

Jacob was already moving, packing gear. "That's what the second cipher was for. Not just the next place—the timing."

They moved fast now. No wasted words. Years of muscle memory activated, silent agreement forming between them like breath in frost.

As they reached the corridor, Nex's voice returned one last time:

"Final message fragment recovered."

They stopped mid-stride.

"Voiceprint: Ethan Goldstein. Timestamp: 01:32 AM local. Content fragment: 'If this reaches you, it means they've already erased the original. What's left... is only the echo.'"

The final projection flickered. Ethan's face appeared—once, twice, then bled into static. But for that moment, she saw him. Not the message. Not the myth. Him.

Hannah didn't speak. Her lips parted, but nothing came out. She looked at Jacob—but she wasn't really seeing him.

Then she moved.

Not like a field agent. Not like a Cedrela operative.

She moved like someone chasing the last heartbeat of someone she wasn't ready to let go.

Hannah didn't speak. She just ran.

—They weren't chasing Ethan's trail anymore. They were running out of time to become it.

Chapter Nineteen - The Geometry of Silence

They arrived at Vault Echo-9 just after dusk. Snow hadn't reached this far south, but the air carried the kind of stillness that didn't belong to anything living. The terrain was scrubbed stone, barren and quiet. Too quiet.

"This was supposed to be off-grid," Jacob said, scanning the ridge. "No one was meant to know it existed."

Hannah stepped forward. The vault's outer shell had once been disguised as a geological observatory—Cedrela's habit of hiding memory where no one looked. But now, the front panel was partially open. The lock had been overridden. The silence wasn't natural. It was surgical.

Jacob moved closer and crouched near the threshold.

"There's no entry trace," he muttered. "Not even residue heat signature. Whoever was here... they were professional. Real professional. They covered their trail so well it's like the door opened itself."

Inside, the air was cold, untouched, sterile. Walls of labeled crates lined the chamber. A dead terminal glowed faintly in sleep mode. The order in the room was almost unsettling—like someone had cleaned up after breaking in.

"Someone's been here," Jacob said again, softer now. "And they knew exactly what not to touch."

Nex blinked to life.

"Archive identifier confirmed. This is Vault Echo-9. Primary logs indicate security breach. Internal log integrity: 48%."

Hem chimed in.

"Motion record fragmented. Last trace accessed: 19 hours ago."

The room hummed faintly with old energy. Hannah moved to the center console and activated Nex's tactile interface. Nex added on.

"Legacy stream detected, partial cache from Ethan Goldstein. Warning: data integrity compromised. Overwrite event logged by Cedrela internal authority."

Jacob's head snapped around. "Cedrela did this?"

"Or someone under its name," Hannah said.

She reached for the reader. The console offered only fragments: Ethan's tone, splintered words. But they were unmistakable.

"This isn't preservation. It's disassembly. What I built wasn't meant to be safe. It was meant to be remembered."

The rest dissolved in static.

There was a sharp edge in her voice when she said, "They came here to erase him."

"No," Jacob said, stepping beside her. "They came here to finish what he couldn't."

Nex pinged.

"Archive echo detected in sublevel containment. Access possible via eastern corridor."

The eastern wing had collapsed years ago—seismic damage, long unreported. They moved cautiously, Hem mapping step by step. The air grew colder. The corridor narrowed. The walls were lined with discarded Cedrela tech—interfaces no longer in use, storage units stacked like forgotten confessionals.

Hannah moved through the space, scanning shelves. She opened three crates—nothing. Old Cedrela comms. Broken prototype interface units. A pulse relay without a power cell.

She turned sharply. "They left decoys."

Jacob nodded, already moving. "We're supposed to waste time in the wrong places."

In the far corner in the final room, tucked beneath a tarp marked DISCARDED: CORRUPTED DATA UNITS, Hannah spotted a steel case—smaller, newer. Out of place.

Hannah found it.

A simple steel case. Locked.

Jacob moved to scan it, but Nex overrode him.

"Manual access required. Legacy print match: Hannah Goldstein."

Hannah reached forward. Her hand hesitated. Not because she doubted it would open—but because she knew what came next would change everything.

The lock clicked. The seal hissed open. No server. No drive. Just a leather-bound notebook, the edges curled, the paper brittle at the corners.

On the first page, Ethan's handwriting.

"If they find this before you, everything collapses. But if you're reading this... go where the echoes last longest."

Jacob leaned closer. "What does that mean?"

Hannah didn't answer. Not immediately.

She was remembering the way Ethan used to walk ahead of her—never too far, just far enough that she always had to catch up. The way he used silence like punctuation. The way he'd pause in museums—not for the exhibits, but for the acoustics.

One night, in Istanbul, they'd wandered through the Sultanahmet district long after curfew. He'd stopped near a locked gate, behind which ancient stone columns vanished into underground darkness.

"Here," he'd whispered. "This is the place where sound remembers longest. Water... walls... time. It all holds."

She hadn't understood then. She did now.

She looked at Jacob, her voice steadier than she felt.

"I know where he meant."

Hannah closed her eyes. She didn't need coordinates.

The wind was picking up outside, but down here, the silence pressed like weight.

Jacob was halfway through encrypting Ethan's notebook scan into Hem's protected memory bank when the vault's proximity alarm triggered—not loudly, just a single pulse.

"Contact on the perimeter," Hem said. "No movement yet. Single source."

Jacob tensed, hand on the grip of the sidearm he rarely used. "Could be Mehmet," he said.

"No," Hannah murmured. "If it was Mehmet, we wouldn't get a warning."

Footsteps echoed before the figure emerged—broad-shouldered, steady gait, no visible weapon.

"Cedrela ID confirmed," Nex said. "Profile match: Elias Roche. Level 4 field operative. Handler class."

Hannah hadn't seen Elias in nearly four years. He'd been Ethan's closest field confidant for a time—before everything started to fracture. When Ethan vanished, it was Elias who first briefed her, who walked her through Cedrela's tactical silence. He was the one who told her not to search too loudly, not to dig too fast. He never said Ethan was dead. He just said Ethan was "on the other side of the signal." She'd never forgiven him for that.

Elias had been inside for hours. Watching? Searching? The implications made Hannah's stomach tighten. Elias stepped into view. Calm. Controlled. Like this meeting had always been part of the plan.

He hadn't just stumbled on the vault. He'd been here—four hours ahead of them. Long enough to scrub his entry, reroute Hem's diagnostics, and plant misdirection like breadcrumbs for the blind. They'd been rerouted. Elias had accessed the vault through a buried Cedrela clearance path no longer on record. He hadn't left because this wasn't a retreat. It was a reckoning. He'd waited—quietly, intentionally—because he knew Ethan's trail would lead her here. And he wanted to be the one waiting at the end of it.

"You shouldn't be here," Elias said calmly, like a parent catching children in a place they didn't belong. "But I expected you'd come anyway."

Hannah didn't move. "Why erase Ethan's voice?"

He sighed. "Because Ethan stopped speaking for Cedrela. And started speaking *against it.* That's not betrayal. That's collapse."

Jacob stepped forward. "Ethan didn't collapse anything. You did."

Elias tilted his head. "You think memory's enough to hold off what's coming? Cedrela is being repurposed. It always was. He knew that. That's why he tried to sabotage the core archive."

"He tried to protect it," Hannah snapped.

"He tried to protect you," Elias corrected. "That's why he made the deal."

Silence fell like snowfall—slow, muffling, deadly.

"What deal?" Jacob asked, but his voice already sounded like he didn't want the answer.

Elias looked only at Hannah.

"With Mehmet. With Orion. Ethan gave partial access to Cedrela's deep systems. Not because he wanted to burn it down—but because he thought it would keep you off the target list."

Hannah's throat tightened. "You're lying."

"No. I'm telling you why your husband died with more enemies than friends."

Hem pulsed red. Nex whispered:

"Digital trace detected. Counter-signature near-identical to Elias Roche. Two overlays. One trace-tied to Cedrela. One to an unverified secondary node. Possible split-agent alignment."

Jacob's hand flexed near his weapon. "You're not just a handler anymore."

"I'm a realist," Elias replied. "And I came here to offer you clarity. Ethan's legacy can't survive both Cedrela and Mehmet. Choose one."

Hannah stared at him. Her pulse was calm. Her voice wasn't.

"I've already made my choice."

She turned her back.

Elias hadn't followed. He didn't shout after them. He didn't raise a weapon. When they reached the stairwell, Hem confirmed it

"No pursuit, no signal. Just a trace left behind in the vault: stationary, alone."

"He's not moving," Nex said.

Elias had stayed in the dark. Maybe to guard what was left. Or maybe because he knew he no longer had anything to chase.

They didn't speak again until they reached the upper chamber.

The corridor behind them felt longer now, as if silence had stretched it on purpose. Hannah carried Ethan's notebook like a fragile relic, the cover still warm from her hand. Jacob walked slightly behind her, his jaw tight, his trust recalibrating.

"Hem," Jacob said quietly, "begin signal suppression. We leave no trail from this point forward."

"Suppression active," Hem confirmed. "No outgoing pulses. No triangulation risk."

FLASHBACK

As they walked the corridor out, the light from behind grew fainter. Her thoughts drifted sideways—back to the early days, when Ethan still smiled at puzzles. When he believed Cedrela was more than secrecy, more than leverage.

She remembered one night on the coast, before Athens—he had set up a candle on a windowsill and asked her to listen to the wind for ten minutes in silence.

"Most people rush to fill quiet," he'd said. "But sometimes, that's when truth slips through."

She hadn't said anything then, but now she whispered his words back into the stone.

"Truth slips through.

They reached the surface. The cold hit like a question.

Hannah looked out across the flat ridgeline. Dusk had fractured into night. Above them, the sky bled stars—clear, pin-sharp. She'd never seen the world so silent.

"We're not done, are we?" Jacob asked.

She shook her head. "No. We're not even close."

She opened the notebook again. On the second-to-last page, Ethan had drawn a crude sketch—a columned space, half-submerged in black water. The ink had run slightly at the edges, but the image was unmistakable.

"This is Istanbul," she said. "The cistern."

Jacob looked over. "That's ancient Cedrela territory. Pre-restructure. Why would he send us there?"

She traced the lines of the sketch with one finger.

"Because some conversations need water and stone. Not wires and firewalls."

They moved quickly. Within the hour, they reached Kars Airport—a two-hour drive off-grid using Hem's rerouted off-road path. They boarded the 10:05 PM flight to Istanbul, their IDs masked beneath dormant Cedrela credentials. No chatter. No digital signature.

They landed in Istanbul just after midnight.

Hem's alert had come just as their plane began its descent into Istanbul. A secure Cedrela burst-ping had been registered less than an hour after they left the vault—an internal routing tied to Elias Roche. It hadn't broadcast a location. Just a signal.

"He warned them," Jacob said quietly. "Or warned him."

Hannah didn't reply. She just looked out the window as the city came into view. "Then let's not arrive silently. Let's arrive listening."

The city between the early hours of one and five was a different Istanbul—half-asleep, half-sacred. They wandered the empty curves of Sultanahmet like ghosts retracing someone else's dream. Streetlamps flickered above cobblestones slick with mist. The Blue Mosque loomed silent behind iron gates, its domes like sentinels guarding the quiet. At a twenty-four-hour café tucked beside an alley near Küçük Ayasofya, they took turns shutting their eyes—one always awake, always watching. Hannah cupped a glass of scalding tea, breathing in the scent of bergamot and steam.

No one asked who they were. No one needed to.

In the stillness, Istanbul revealed itself—not in the call to prayer or the rush of trams, but in the hush of shuttered shops, the curve of old stone steps, the scent of sea salt carried uphill. Time moved differently here. Slower. Gentler. As if the city had learned that certain truths only arrived in silence. And that some kinds of remembering could only happen when the world forgot to speak.

By dawn, they were standing outside the Basilica Cistern.

Sultanahmet was hushed in the early hour. Mist curled through the streets. The entrance to the Basilica was closed to the public, but Nex had already infiltrated the permit system and flagged a private inspection for restoration.

They passed through the threshold alone.

Below, the columns rose like ghost trees out of the still water. Orange lighting cast reflections that shimmered without movement. The Basilica Cistern had been built in the 6th century under Emperor Justinian I, the same Emperor who commisioned the Hagia Sophia—an answer not to prayer, but to power. It wasn't a church. It was infrastructure masquerading as sacred space. Nearly 10,000 slaves labored beneath Constantinople to create it, carving out a chamber that could hold over 80,000 cubic meters of water—enough to quench the demands of an empire and the excesses of a palace.

336 marble columns rose from the water like petrified memories. Some bore the carved scrolls of Corinthian influence, others were scavenged from older ruins—pagan temples broken and repurposed to feed a Christian throne. Light and shadow played across their slick surfaces like echoes from another world.

During the Ottoman era, the cistern was largely forgotten—relegated to myth and occasional use by palace kitchens. It wasn't rediscovered until the 16th century, when a scholar noticed locals fishing from their basements. Even now, in the age of ticket booths and controlled entry, the air here felt unchanged—thick with breath from centuries past.

Its columns didn't just hold a ceiling. They held weight. Secrets. Regret. The kind of silence that could only be engineered by empires—and remembered by those who outlasted them.

Hannah descended first, her boots soft against the damp stone. Jacob followed.

They stopped near the Medusa head.

"Why here?" he asked.

She didn't answer.

She reached into her coat and pulled out the notebook again. There, tucked between the pages, was a card—one she hadn't seen before.

It bore one word.

"Listen."

She looked around. Listened.

No sound.

Then Nex's voice—barely above a whisper.

"Encrypted signal embedded in acoustic feedback. Audio pattern matches Ethan Goldstein encryption. Final archive pending retrieval."

She turned to Jacob. "He didn't leave a message."

He frowned. "What, then?"

She stared out over the still water.

—"He left a place. One where the silence could speak for him."

Chapter Twenty - The Last Conversation

The sound of their footsteps softened as they descended.

Beneath the city, the air changed. It wasn't damp—it was listening. Stone absorbed their presence like memory absorbs touch. Each step Hannah took toward the chamber at the cistern's end felt less like a path and more like a ritual. She could feel the history here—not the kind taught in books, but the kind buried under silence.

"You should go no further," she said to Jacob, pausing at a grated partition.

He looked at her, hesitant.

"If he's already there, you'll be outnumbered."

She shook her head. "This won't be a fight."

She passed through the opening alone. As they approached the lower threshold of the cistern, Hannah paused. She turned to Jacob, voice low.

"You'll stay hidden."

He didn't argue. Just activated Hem's silent drone-mode—visual feed only, no pulse. Nex was already dormant, masked to avoid legacy trace interference. Jacob stepped back, fading into the shadows above. The mission was no longer surveillance. It was witness.

"Ten minutes," he said. "Then I come down."

The chamber was darker here. The water shallower. Reflections flickered, fractured. At the centre, beneath a low arch of Roman brick, stood a man with his back to her—coat folded over one arm, no weapon visible, no guards in sight.

Mehmet Orman – He was taller than she remembered from surveillance stills—lean, deliberate, cut from the kind of discipline that didn't need noise to command space. His hair was black, streaked with frost at the temples, not from age but from sleepless calculation. His face was clean-shaven, angular, yet softened by the calm of someone who believed composure was the greatest weapon.

He wore a coat the color of dried blood—dark wool, no insignia. Underneath, a grey collar, sharp as a blade. No weapon on his belt. No visible comms. Just a ring on his right index finger—Cedrela black, but inverted. Memory not as preservation, but as leverage.

His eyes were the most dangerous part: not angry, not cold, but measured. The eyes of a man who had read too many classified truths and started to believe they made him immune to consequence. The kind who didn't destroy archives because he hated the past—but because he feared what it might resurrect.

He turned before she spoke. Not with surprise, but with expectation. As though he'd always known she would walk this far, and perhaps, no farther.

"You've come," he said simply.

She didn't answer. She moved closer, her boots careful on the slick stone.

"Did he send you here?" Mehmet asked.

"No," she said. "He led me here."

There was a pause. He smiled faintly, tiredly.

"There's a difference."

He gestured to the far end of the chamber—a wide, shallow basin surrounded by stone columns. The acoustics made every word stretch longer than its echo. Water dripped somewhere in the distance, a near-constant murmur beneath their breath.

"Ethan told you I was the enemy?"

"He didn't have to," she said. "You called yourself that when you offered to erase him."

Mehmet exhaled through his nose. Not quite a laugh.

"I offered to keep what was left."

He stepped closer, voice low.

"You think he was trying to save Cedrela. He wasn't. He was trying to buy time—for you. He knew Cedrela couldn't survive what it had become. He gave me access because he knew you wouldn't surrender to it—but you might be consumed by it."

Silence again. Then he added, almost gently:

"He made that deal knowing you'd hate him for it."

Hannah's pulse was steady. But her chest ached like someone had spoken through her bones.

"Why are you really here?" she asked.

"To finish the question," Mehmet said. "And let you answer it."

He reached into his coat and pulled out a small, dark case.

"This contains the remaining Cedar Key signature. Give me Nex—and I'll release it. Ethan's memory survives in our version of history. Safe. Sanitised. But remembered."

"And if I don't?" she asked.

He tilted his head.

"Then he's erased. Clean. No myth. No memory. Just data fragments rotting inside corrupted nodes."

This chamber had likely heard negotiations like this before. In Byzantine times, it would have been a sanctuary from spies—an unofficial vault where generals whispered about uprisings and advisors plotted how to keep empires from crumbling. Even in the Ottoman era, Hannah imagined it repurposed in shadows—secret exchanges under the veil of damp stone and water that forgot. What they were doing now wasn't new. It was just older than memory.

Above the chamber, Jacob stayed crouched in the high alcove behind a maintenance gate—eyes on Hem's wrist interface. The feed was dark-mode, no light, no pulse. Just lines of thermal mapping and acoustic feedback. Mehmet's voice echoed low through the cistern, but it wasn't the only signal Hem caught.

> "Sub-audible ping detected," Hem whispered in Jacob's ear. "Encrypted Cedrela fallback trigger. Origin: secondary chamber, east column grid."

Jacob's jaw tightened. Mehmet hadn't come alone. Or if he had, he didn't intend to leave that way.

He tapped a silent command—divert Nex's uplink queue and shield Hannah's position from Cedrela's legacy satellite trace. If Mehmet activated his contingency, Jacob would trigger theirs.

Mehmet placed the case on the stone ledge between them. It didn't echo. It just sat there, like a verdict that hadn't decided who was guilty yet.

"This isn't a threat," he said. "It's a mercy."

Hannah didn't move. "That's what tyrants always say."

He almost smiled. "And yet you came."

"I came to hear the end of a story," she said. "Not rewrite the beginning."

Mehmet stepped back, pacing slowly—just one line, from one column to another. His voice softened.

"You've seen what Cedrela became. Ethan couldn't stop that. He saw how it changed. You did too. And in the end... he gave me the keys. Because he knew memory, left unguarded, becomes myth. And myth, if weaponised, is worse than forgetting."

Hannah stared at the black case. Inside was the last Cedrela system imprint, the final safeguard. A sanitized version of Ethan's legacy—or the erasure of it all.

"You can give me Nex," Mehmet continued. "We embed Ethan in the official records—washed, rounded, remembered. The myth becomes manageable. Your name survives with it. Or..."

"Or I walk," she said.

He nodded. "And he disappears. Every trace. Every instance. Every whisper."

She didn't flinch. She just took one slow step forward.

"If you could erase him," she said, "you would've already."

Mehmet tilted his head, faintly impressed. "Then let's hear him."

The words hung there—curious, commanding, mocking.

Hannah didn't speak. She reached slowly into her coat and pulled out the notebook—Ethan's.

Tucked inside was the card. Just one word.

"Listen."

She didn't look at Mehmet. She didn't speak to Nex.

She whispered the word into the room.

"Listen."

The chamber held the sound like breath. And then the water near the basin vibrated—just once.

Nex powered up, breaking his dormancy without instruction. A pulse emitted, invisible, harmonic. The encryption key was not text. It was tone.

"Voiceprint matched," Nex said. "Final Ethan Goldstein archive: initializing."

The acoustics shifted.

A voice began to rise from the columns—not through a speaker, but through the air itself. Echo first. Then clarity.

The voice came slowly—first as echo, then as presence. Not broadcast. Not clean. But deliberate. Like a thought formed too carefully to be rushed.

"If you're hearing this, it means you've reached the end. But not the edge."

Ethan's voice didn't sound like a message. It sounded like a man standing just behind her, somewhere between memory and meaning.

"I didn't leave a legacy. I left questions. Cedrela stopped asking them."

The light in the cistern dimmed as if the water itself was listening.

"Mehmet is right about one thing. I gave him access. Not because I trusted him—but because I didn't trust the silence that followed me. If I could protect you, Hannah, by becoming the villain... then that was a cost I knew you'd understand."

Hannah closed her eyes.

"But this isn't about what I gave up. It's about what you choose to carry."

He paused. The silence pressed in again.

"Cedrela wasn't corrupted from outside. It calcified from within. From caution. From fear. From forgetting that truth is fragile because it's alive."

A tremor ran through the columns.

"If you give Nex to them, they'll remember a version of me I never became. If you walk away, they'll try to erase me. But either way, Hannah... I don't want to be archived. I want to be remembered. Not for how I ended—but for how I listened."

She gripped the notebook tighter and looked at Mehmet, but he didn't move. Not yet.

"If you still believe in what we began... then don't finish it. Rewrite it."

The voice faded—not cut, but closed, like a book put down with care.

Nex blinked.

"Final message complete. No additional audio. Trace wiped."

Silence reclaimed the chamber. Not hollow—just full of something too deep for sound.

Mehmet stepped forward. "You've made your point. Now make the trade."

Hannah stepped back from the basin. Her hands didn't shake. Her breath did. She didn't answer. She stared at him for a full beat—then walked past the case without touching it.

She turned toward Mehmet, who stood unmoving, unreadable.

"You walk out with him," Mehmet warned, "and Cedrela won't just come for you. It will hunt you. What Ethan built will become a ghost story."

"You're right," she said. "He's gone. But not the way you planned."

She walked past him, notebook in hand, Nex silent in her coat.

"Where are you going?" Mehmet asked.

She paused only once.

"Some conversations," she said, "never end. They simply echo louder—until someone listens."

And then she walked into the light.

The light above was brighter now. Dawn spilled into the city like quiet absolution. Outside, Istanbul stirred—tourists had begun to gather—cameras slung over shoulders, headphones chirping in a dozen languages. The cistern would be open within the hour.

As Hannah and Jacob approached the gates, a ripple moved through the crowd. Two men stepped from either side of the exit path—too tidy, too timed. Clean jackets. Comms tucked in their collars.

Jacob didn't break stride.

"Hannah. Right side. Hem is live."

Mehmet's voice thundered behind them, sharper now, projecting authority.

"That woman is carrying stolen encrypted data. She is in violation of—"

A third man, dressed like museum staff, moved to block their path. Hannah braced, but Jacob was already moving. He tapped Hem's interface—fast, silent, surgical.

Within seconds, the museum's internal security feed began cycling through old footage. Mehmet's Cedrela credentials lit up on the security log—falsified, redirected to a flagged identity batch marked for international surveillance review.

Hem wasn't just hiding them—he was making Mehmet look like the breach. His Cedrela ID now mirrored flagged trace signatures—like a diplomatic alias gone rogue. To the museum's system, he was no longer an officer. He was a red alert.

Hem pulsed in Jacob's ear:

"Decoy uploaded. All queries now route back to Mehmet's ID as potential intruder."

A sharp whistle came from the front kiosk. One of the museum guards turned.

"Hey! You—stop right there!"

Mehmet looked stunned. The two men flanking Hannah and Jacob hesitated—confused. The guard was moving now—toward Mehmet.

"You don't have clearance here. Hands where I can see them!"

"What?" Mehmet's voice cracked. "I'm with Central Access—Cedrela—I—"

The guard didn't care.

Jacob slipped his hand into Hannah's.

"Now," he said.

They disappeared sideways—down a back passage Nex had mapped in advance, where a catering delivery truck blocked the view from the front gate. They passed through the shadow, down a narrow alley scented with simit and diesel and early-morning tea.

No one followed.

No one called out.

Mehmet's voice was lost behind them in a rising sea of static and contradiction.

They emerged four streets east, where the air was cooler and quieter. Istanbul stirred gently now, the way cities do when stories have shifted just beneath the surface.

"Some conversations," Hannah whispered, "never end."

"They just find better listeners," Jacob said.

—They walked into the sun—Jacob's arm across Hannah's shoulders, quiet and steady, like a promise no one needed to say aloud.

Epilogue - New Beginnings

The sun breached the edge of the Bosphorus with the kind of quiet glory that made Istanbul feel eternal. Along the waterline, ferries stirred, slow and purposeful. The calls of gulls tangled with the scent of brewing tea and coal smoke. The city moved not with urgency—but with memory.

Hannah stood alone on the rooftop of their temporary flat in Bebek, coat drawn around her, the violin case resting beside her like an unopened letter. The notebook was already packed. So was the pendant. She didn't need them in her hands anymore.

She had already arranged the next place—new keys, new name, new silence. Mehmet wouldn't stop looking. Not yet. Not until Cedrela had rewritten every echo. So for now, she would stay ahead of the noise.

She looked out across the Bosphorus, its current slow but unrelenting. Somewhere beneath the surface, truths passed between continents. Between languages. Between lives.

She opened the locket.

Inside, the tulip glowed in the morning light—red against brass, worn smooth by time and weather and grief.

She didn't cry.

Not this time.

She just smiled, as if Ethan had said something only she could hear.

From the street below came the ordinary rhythm of life: a shopkeeper unlocking his shutter. A boy chasing pigeons. A woman humming the opening notes of a song no one had recorded.

And somewhere in it all, Hannah heard the last message.

Not from Ethan.

Not from Jacob.

But from herself.

A promise, not to archive what was lost—but to carry what still burned.

—"Cedrela... isn't silence. It's what silence guards."

About the Author

Soraya Radfield is the pen name of a globe-trotting writer with a deep passion for ancient history and the emotional undercurrents that shape human stories. With over 25 years of experience in Project Planning and Cost Control across multiple industries and continents, she brings a unique lens of precision, depth, and cultural curiosity to her fiction.

Her debut novel, The Last Conversation, weaves suspense, sentiment, and history into a richly layered journey inspired by the thousand-year legacy of the Ottoman Empire. Drawing influence from historians and their own travels through Istanbul, Georgia, Armenia, and Eastern Europe, Soraya crafts a narrative that invites readers to uncover what history leaves behind—and what emotions survive it.

Known for her evocative style in the genre of Emotive Suspense Drama, Soraya writes in the quiet cocoon of her dedicated space, with background music and a trusted laptop that helps her tune out the world and step fully into her stories. She hopes readers walk away from her novels not only moved by the characters, but also carrying new insights about the places and histories she loves.

The Last Conversation marks the beginning of Soraya's writing journey. She is currently working on her next novel, Echoes of the Empire, a historical fiction project that explores ancient trade, spiritual echoes, and soul-bound legacies across time.

A Note from the Author

Thank you for joining me on this journey through *The Last Conversation*. If this story moved you, sparked curiosity, or brought a fragment of history to life, I would be deeply grateful if you shared your thoughts with others.

Leave a Review

Your honest review on **Amazon, Goodreads,** or your favourite book platform helps new readers discover this story and helps authors like me keep writing. Even a few words can make a big difference.

Let's Stay Connected

To hear about future releases, behind-the-scenes content, or get a first look at *Echoes of the Empire*, follow me online or sign up for updates at:

http://amazon.com/author/soraya_radfield.23

Goodreads: [Your Goodreads link]

Instagram / TikTok / FB / Twitter: @sorayaradfield

Book Clubs & Discussion Groups

If your book club or group is reading *The Last Conversation*, I'd love to hear from you. Reach out via my website for discussion guides and special appearances.

Thank you for reading and remembering the stories hidden in silence.

— *Soraya Radfield*